Silence Rides Alone

by Charles Millsted

Pat + John

Many thanks,

Charles

Silence Rides Alone by Charles Millsted
Copyright© 2016 Charles Millsted
Cover Design Livia Reasoner
Sundown Press
www.sundownpress.com

SUNDOWN PRESS

All rights reserved.
ISBN-13: 978-1533388223
ISBN-10: 1533388229

This is a work of fiction. The characters, incidents, and dialogues are products of the author's imagination and are not to be construed as real.

No part of this book may be used or reproduced in any manner whatsoever without written permission of the publisher, except in the case of brief quotations embodied in critical articles and reviews.

Chapter One

The two covered wagons creaked slowly to a halt at the signal of the lone rider ahead of them. He rode casually halfway back to them and shouted.

"Okay, Nuts-bums. You can unhitch the horses to drink here. Last bit of water for a while."

Jacob Nussbaum held back his annoyance at the continued mispronunciation of his family name. He felt sure it was done deliberately. He signalled his brother in the rear wagon to let the horses loose to drink and asked the women to prepare food. The routine was well practised by now, near as they were to the end of their journey. Jacob looked up to the high hills beyond which lay the land they had bought. Finally, the end. The adults of the family group had crossed the best part of two continents and an ocean to get this far. Even the children, true Americans, born in the claustrophobic squalor of New York City, had travelled nearly two thousand miles.

Jacob looked around at his extended family. He noticed Manny, his eldest at fourteen, running after the dog that had travelled with them since St. Louis. Encouraged by the scent of some rabbit or prairie dog it was easily out-pacing the boy. Jacob breathed in deeply. This was how it should be—the freedom for children to run in the wide open spaces.

****

"Louis," called Manny, having lost sight of the dog in the tall prairie grass. The boy stopped running and tried to listen out. Louis seemed to have picked Manny out from the moment they saw him scrounging around the wagons in St. Louis. At his father's request, he'd spent a day walking him about the town to try and find the owner. By the end of the day, they'd failed to find the original owner, but had succeeded in becoming fast friends. Manny waited for his breathing to slow down so that he could listen better. He believed the dog would come to him in time and, sure enough, he saw a rustle of grass moments before he saw the dog itself bounding up to him.

"Good dog," Manny said. "Best get back now. We've run pretty far from the wagons."

Just as Manny stood and turned, ready to retrace his steps to the wagons, he heard a sound he recognised from the times when Carlson, the guide, had ridden off trail to hunt something to supplement the evening meals. Gunfire. Manny started running even before the recognition of the sound fully registered. Louis loped alongside him as if he sensed a need to stay together. More shots rang out as Manny's body defied his efforts to run ever faster.

****

The same sounds of gunfire were a faint whisper on the wind by the time they reached J.T. Silence. To many, they would have blended into the background murmurs of birdsong and animal life—but his years in the army, and the life he'd led since, had left him all too familiar with those deathly echoes.

He was still up near the rim of the valley and had already spotted the tracks of a small wagon party half-a-day's travel ahead. Easy pickings for outlaws, perhaps; but at the same time, likely to be so poor as to be hardly worthwhile. He slid off his horse and walked it down the trail. If there was trouble ahead, he'd rather meet it on a horse with fresh legs.

****

Louis whimpered by the lifeless body of Marta, the girl who'd fed him titbits of food while helping her mother prepare meals. Manny was on his knees, holding her head. He was too numbed, too much in shock, to even cry. All dead. His mother, father, brother, uncle, aunt, cousins. Everyone. Marta was furthest from the wagons. That, and the mangled mess which had been her torso, suggested that she'd tried to run but had been shot in the back.

Manny had feared the worst when he'd seen smoke rising while still only half-way back to the wagons. He looked around at the smouldering husks of the wagons. The horses had all been stolen.

It had taken him a few minutes to realise that Carlson was not among the dead bodies. His first, foolish thought was that he had been taken prisoner…but then, the likely truth dawned on him.

Manny looked among the half-burned box of farm tools the family had bought with the wagons. He took a spade that had been singed but was still basically sound. Walking to a patch of ground that had no apparent rocks, he thrust the spade into the dirt. Finally, the tears came. He fell to his knees again and hugged the spade handle…and sobbed. Louis came to stand by him, but made no sound.

****

The approach of dusk did little to lower the baking temperature on the plains as Silence, patting the Henry rifle strapped to his saddle bag, approached the burnt-out wagons. His horse had likely caught the scent of the dead bodies before they were in sight. Silence was sure any raiders were long gone but approached with caution, none the less. There was a fair chance some of the larger scavenging critters hereabouts had arrived on the scene, by now.

Silence rode a measured circle around the husks of the two wagons. On the far side, he saw that someone had dragged the bodies underneath a tree. Whoever had done so had attempted to dig graves, but had succeeded only in scooping out enough topsoil to create shallow graves a few inches deep into which the corpses had been placed. Whoever it was had then shovelled the topsoil back over. Silence counted eight shapes. He knew that scavengers would dig through the meager protection and into the bodies before the sun came up the next day.

The other odd thing Silence noticed was that the raiders seemed to have taken only the horses. There was evidence of mindless death and destruction, but no sign of looting. The few items of any value these people appeared to have had were still there. A box of tools had been scattered, but looked complete. Silence found a woman's tidy box behind the seat of the lead wagon. Inside were some bead necklaces of a type which could be traded for furs with most Indian tribes. There was also a small silver chain. Clearly, this had been an assassination rather than the opportunistic raid he had expected.

The ground ahead of the wagons showed tracks of several horses. Three, perhaps four, had ridden in. More had ridden out –that accounted for the horses from the wagons. He found, also, the footprints of a survivor imprinted over the top of the horses' tracks. Small feet suggested a woman or youth. There were also dog prints in the softer ground near the ford. Too few for a pack, so perhaps domesticated. If it belonged to the survivor, it might lead him to the raiders—which was not likely to be the best way to stay alive.

Silence toyed with the idea of burying the bodies properly, but doing so would mean leaving the survivor, possibly a lone woman, on their own out there. He watered his horse and rode off, following the trail west.

Chapter Two

Silence heard a dog bark in the darkness ahead. It had taken him three hours to catch up, and he admitted to himself that he was impressed with the progress the survivor had made. The muffled sound of a human voice quietening the dog gave away their position as just a stone's throw ahead. Close enough.

"My name is J.T. Silence," he called out. "I'm not an enemy or looking for any trouble. I saw what happened back there. I can help you."

The dog barked again, but there was no reply from the human voice. Silence continued. "That's okay. Take your time. It's too late and too dark to ride further. I'm making camp here. I've got cold beef jerky and some hot coffee once I get a fire going. I'm willing to share both. Come up when you're ready."

Silence stepped down from his horse which stood close without needing to be tethered. From the saddle, he unhooked a bag of firewood and kindling which he kept ready for the times he had to make camp after dark. He pulled a small tinder box from inside his jacket and set about starting a fire, all the time keeping a watch to see when the survivor would venture forward. By the time Silence had begun heating a metal pot of coffee he heard a tentative voice.

"Sir." The call was that of a youth not a woman. A boy whose voice was not quite fully broken. Silence waited as the youth edged forward into the small glow of light thrown out by the fire. The dog padded by the boy's side.

"I don't know if you were calling to me or someone else but you offered help, and I think I need it," the young man said.

"Sit here and rest, lad. There's some jerky wrapped in that

cloth your dog's already sniffing. Take some for each of you."

The youth ripped some off and gave it to his dog before taking some for himself. "Can I trust you?" he asked.

"You already have, boy. If I wanted to kill you or some such there's not much you could do to stop me; but nor do you have anything I want. You're as safe here as anywhere, and my offer of help was genuine."

Silence noticed the boy shivering. Fear or cold—couldn't blame him for either.

"I saw what happened to your family. I can't put that right, but I can help you get to a safe place."

"Thank you."

"What's your name, boy?"

"Manny. It's short for Emanuel."

"I'm J.T. It's just short."

Silence noticed a half-smile from the boy. He passed him a cup of coffee to wash down the jerky as well as to get some warmth inside young Manny's body.

"I was trying to follow the murderers," Manny said.

"I thought you might've been. Dog, there, probably helped. You were doing pretty well. Probably *too* well." Silence noticed the boy stop in mid-sip as he said this. "Tell me, Manny, what would you have done if you'd caught up with them?"

"I don't know," Manny said with his head facing down to the ground. "I think our trail guide betrayed us to the killers. His name is Carlson."

"The tracks by the wagons showed he rode off with them at a pace. Suggests he didn't need persuading to go with them. What we need to do is get you to a town with a lawman where you can tell your story. Let them sort out this Carlson."

Silence judged that the food and drink had revived the boy enough for his senses to register the exhaustion he must be feeling.

"Best sleep now, boy. The fire will keep any four-legged pests away, and my rifle will deter any two-legged ones."

****

By the time Manny woke the next morning, J.T. had already packed up his few things and was spreading out the last dying embers of the fire. J.T. handed him a canteen of water and some more jerky. Manny chewed the food and watched J.T. saddle the horse. His manner was assured; not in the brash way that Carlson had been, but calmer. The odd grey hair showed up in stark contrast to the darkness of the rest.

"My horse can carry us both as far as a farm where I know some good people. Old Joan makes a good stew. You can only go so far before you tire of jerky."

They rode without talking for a while. Manny concentrated on sitting right in the saddle. The more he tried to keep straight, the more he got bounced. He tried relaxing instead, concentrating on the sights and sounds around him; shrill bird, animal noises and the sway of the few trees in the light breeze. The ground looked like it was already baking in the morning sun. Manny wondered why his father had brought them out here, but he also remembered the two small rooms in New York that eight of them had shared and the smell of the streets. He remembered, too, the names they had been called; the names his mother had been called.

"Where are you travelling to, Mr. Silence?" Manny asked, breaking the quiet.

"I'm looking to meet up with someone I heard had come this way."

When Silence added nothing further, Manny tried to continue the conversation. "We were headed to a valley called White River to start a farm on land my father and uncle had bought between them."

Silence didn't know the area ahead well, but could guess that a valley called White River was so called because of the effect of the rocks and the gradient on the water. *Would have made ploughing tough. No reason now, though, to disillusion the boy.* "Your father had nearly got you there. See that row of hills ahead? Joan's place is this side just before it starts to rise steeply. If I remember the maps I've seen correctly, then your valley is on the far side of the same hills. Of course, the trails take you the long way round, through a town called Madison Springs."

They both fell back to riding along quietly as the range of hills loomed ever larger ahead of them. The sun had risen close to its mid-day ascendancy when the distant sound of gunfire—one single shot—reached their ears. The sound came from the direction of Joan's farm.

Chapter Three

Four riders reined their horses to a halt under cover of the evergreens that clustered along the foothills of the higher range. They tied the horses to one of the lower branches and walked quietly toward the open space ahead of them.

The largest of the four signalled them to a halt. "Here's where we earn the second half of our money, boys."

"Two old women," snorted a shorter man with reddish hair visible below his hat. "Easy money, McCoy."

"One's not so old by the look of her." The man furthest forward spoke quietly while maintaining his hawk-like vigilance on the farm in front of him. His narrow eyes had picked out the form of a woman washing her clothes in the rocky stream that ran bisecting the distance between the main farm building and where the four men hid. "How about it, McCoy? Do we get to have a little fun, too?"

"We're getting paid to make life unpleasant for 'em. How we do it's up to us." McCoy scanned the terrain casually. "Cal, Turner, fan out to the left." The redhead and the narrow-eyed man picked up their rifles. "Carlson, come in from the right."

****

Cassie looked down at the pile of laundry that still needed scrubbing. Hard work held no fears for her, but the cool feel of the water on her arms made it tempting to take a few minutes and have a swim. She picked up the next shirt and promised herself the swim as a reward, once she was done.

She felt she was being watched before she heard the rifle being cocked. Standing on a rock on the other side of the stream was a lean, narrow-faced man with both his gun and his eyes trained on Cassie.

"Good day to you, miss. I just wanted to let you know that any minute now, you're gonna hear a whole lot of noise, and I didn't want you getting upset by any of it or doing something foolish like running into a bullet." He looked her up from toe to head and back as he spoke. "But, don't worry. There's no need for anybody to get badly hurt."

Gunfire sounded from back near the farm. Cassie thought of her mother, Joan, and started climbing the bank to head back. The hawk-faced man was across the stream and on her before she reached the top.

"Now, missie, doesn't sound like it's entirely safe back there. Why don't you just stay here with me?" He pulled her back down the bank and straddled her. He held the rifle in his right hand as he reached for her blouse buttons with his left. He yanked at the top one with enough force to pull loose the second button as well. Her arms still free, Cassie responded by punching the man in the throat. He recoiled back before looking at Cassie venomously. The assailant then gripped his rifle as though he were about to bring the butt crashing down on Cassie's face when the barrel of a second rifle was pressed up against his cheek.

"Just set the gun down gently," J.T. Silence said. His voice was calm, but suggested suppressed anger. The man put the rifle down to one side. "Now, stand up and let the lady be about her own business."

The hawk-faced man stepped back from Cassie, who was pulling the two sides of her blouse together.

"Thanks, J.T. It's been too long. In fact, just five minutes earlier would have been even better." She stood up and tried to get her breath back. "I need to get back to Ma. There was gunfire."

"We heard it, too. Pick up his gun, Cassie, and let's go and see what's going on."

Cassie was about to ask who 'we' meant when she saw a youthful boy crouching by the side of a dog in the background.

Silence pushed the failed assailant ahead of him toward the

open area in front of the farm house. He indicated for Manny to stay back with the horse. Cassie picked up the rifle and walked a little behind Silence. It looked to Manny like she knew what she was doing with a gun.

As the group got close enough to see the farm buildings, they could see that both the main house and the barn had been shot at. Two men stood with their backs to them looking down at an older woman on the ground. Silence kicked his hostage's legs out from under him so the man collapsed to the ground.

"Watch him," he whispered to Cassie.

"Turn around and drop the guns," Silence called out loudly enough for the gunmen to hear.

Clearly surprised, the two men turned to face Silence. They could also see that Cassie had their comrade under gunpoint. The bigger of the two smiled grimly as he looked directly at Silence. He dropped his gun casually. His red-headed companion did likewise.

"Can we help you, friend?" said McCoy, the big man.

"Maybe," replied Silence. "I know I got two friends here in these two good ladies, so I guess if you're my friend, too, then you'll be happy to explain how you didn't mean them any harm and just what the hell you're doing on their land."

McCoy shrugged. "Doesn't sound like we are friends, after all. Too bad." As soon as he said this, a shot came from the trees at the perimeter of the open space.

Silence felt the bullet bite through his left arm. *Damn. Four not three.* He held onto his rifle, knowing that the two gunmen were as aware as he was that while he might still shoot with just his right arm he stood little chance of doing so with any accuracy. Silence glanced about to take in the wider situation. The two men were bending down to pick up their guns. A further bullet from the hidden gunman had kicked up dust by Cassie's feet forcing her back under cover and allowing the hostage to run. Events had swung in the favour of the raiders. Silence feared the worst. Gunfire came from a new direction; this time, toward the two gunmen who began to retreat back to the cover of the trees. Silence shot his own gun, as accurately as he could with one hand, in the direction of the gunman in the trees. Cassie, from relative safety behind a horse trough, was also now also firing into the clump of trees.

Silence signalled for her to stop. There was no sound of returning gunfire. Manny ran forward with a pistol held tightly in both hands. Louis ran as close to his feet as he could without tripping him.

"I'm sorry I missed them, Mr. Silence, but this gun is heavy and I couldn't aim very well. I found it in your saddle bag." Manny let the pistol relax in his hands so it pointed to the ground. "I saw four men ride off."

"You probably did best in helping to drive them off," Silence said.

Joan was now standing. Silence could see new bruises forming on her face.

"Personally," Joan said, "I'd have been happy if you'd killed them all."

Manny's dog ran round to each of them in turn: Cassie holding her blouse together; Joan feeling her bruises, Manny shaking as he looked around for somewhere to put the gun and Silence, himself, still bleeding from his upper left arm.

"I'm not sure they left because we drove them off," Cassie said. "I think we may hear more from them."

****

"I love you to bits J.T., and you're the son I never had, but sometimes life gets too interesting when you're around," Joan said. She pulled the bandage tight on Silence's arm and tied it securely.

Manny looked around at the inside of the farmhouse. It was basic, but more like a home than any he'd known for a long time in his life. He felt he could fall asleep in the chair in which he sat.

"Those men are nothing to do with me," Silence replied. "They attacked the wagons of the boy's family. Killed all the others. Took nothing except the horses. You got any idea why they might also attack your farm?"

"We've got precious little, and they didn't seem like they were trying to take anything even before you arrived. We've no enemies that I know of."

"I'll go and see your sheriff tomorrow, if you don't mind putting us up for the night."

"I'd mind if you *didn't* stay," Joan said.

"We'd both mind," Cassie added.

"Thanks," J.T. said. "I told the boy your stew was something special."

Joan laughed lightly. "Well, we'll see if I can't live up to your promises, J.T."

Chapter Four

Manny watched as Louis ran round the area in front of the main farmhouse. The dog was enjoying the new morning and the opportunity to sniff where animals might have been in the night. He ran from the wood pile to the well and on to the outhouse, sniffing round the edges of each before returning to start all over again.

"You're good with that dog," Joan said from behind Manny. He'd not heard her. "How long you had him?"

"Since we left St. Louis. That's why I called him Louis. I don't know what he was called before. I looked all over for his owner but he just stayed with me."

"Sometimes a dog chooses who it wants to be with," Joan said. "They're good judges of character, too, so you must be alright. 'Course, having J.T. vouch for you goes heavily in your favour, too."

Joan sipped from a mug of coffee she had brought out with her and sat down on the step of the open porch.

"J.T. and Cassie are fixing some eggs for breakfast." Joan smiled at Manny. "Probably talking some, too."

"Have you known Mr. Silence long?" Manny asked.

"As long as he's been alive. His father had a ranch neighbouring ours in Missouri. He and Cassie were playmates as young 'uns. J.T.'s father sent him off to college when he was eighteen, and he came back three years later with lots of new ways to work the land smarter, and a pretty young bride, as well.

"After a while, his father died, but his wife had a son. That's the way of it, I suppose. He ran the farm well, and seemed happy. Then the Civil War came. Both sides came to our town trying to persuade folks to join up. They were polite at first; then, not so friendly.

"My husband wanted no part of the whole thing, and we pulled up sticks and came out here so he wouldn't have to kill anyone. He died our second winter out here. J.T. went off to join the army in the North. Got to be an officer, and won some medals.

"When he came back, he found his mother, wife and child dead. The farm had been raided by outlaws; deserters in the last months of the war. J.T. swore he'd track down every single one. That was five years ago. I don't make a point of asking him much about what he does, but J.T. has always been good at finishing what he started. I pray he has."

Manny patted Louis, who had joined them while Joan had been talking.

"I'm telling you all this because he probably won't," Joan said. "And best not to say much about it unless he talks first. He's visited us here a few times over the years; always on his own. It's not just for your sake that I'm pleased he stopped to help you."

Cassie came out to call them in for breakfast. J.T. and Joan made small talk about the running of the farm while Louis watched carefully for any titbits that might drop from the table. Manny noticed that Cassie often looked at J.T., even when Joan was talking.

"Who's the sheriff in Madison Springs now?" J.T. asked when the conversation hit a lull.

"Denis Bolton," Cassie said. "Got elected last year."

"Didn't get my vote," Joan chipped in. "Too well padded to my eye. Folks like him well enough in town, but he don't like getting on a horse much—and we don't see him at all at the farms outside of the town."

"I'm due to meet someone in town and I'll need to take the boy, here, to the sheriff so he can report what happened to his family. I'll tell him what happened here, as well."

****

Cassie waited with an empty bucket as J.T. wound the winch, with his good arm, to bring the fresh water up.

"This person you're meeting in Madison Springs. Is that likely to be friendly business?" Cassie asked.

"Don't worry. It'll be peaceful. Captain Hawton sent me a message to meet him there."

Cassie nodded noncommittally but wondered. She'd met Captain Hawton once, and it was true that he was a peaceable gentleman, and genial too. Surprisingly so, for a man that had lost the use of his legs. She also knew that Silence often seemed to go riding off to less friendly appointments after his meetings with Hawton. She didn't know what their professional relationship was, exactly, but that didn't stop her speculating.

"Don't you ever get tired of always being on the move?" Cassie asked.

J.T. poured the water from the winch bucket into the domestic one.

"I'm not ready to stop yet, but the time will come. Soon, I hope."

Chapter Five

Ignoring Joan's claims that his arm needed more time before he used it to ride his horse, J.T. rode into Madison Springs the next day. Manny rode with him; this time, on a pony Cassie had saddled up for him. Joan had offered to look after Louis who was already working his way through the leftovers from breakfast.

Manny was nearer to the ground on the pony than he had been riding behind J.T., and he was grateful for that. His initial apprehension at being in charge of his own steed was soon allayed. The pony was a placid animal, and followed the lead of J.T.'s horse. J.T. himself was clearly not in a talkative mood.

Manny noticed he'd not said much, except for occasional farm talk with Joan, since he'd been to fetch water with Cassie the previous afternoon. If Manny's mother had been here, she would told have both J.T. and Cassie that they should be married. They obviously felt for each other, but Manny could see that J.T. was driven by other things. He thought on the conversation he'd had with Joan and wondered if J.T. was pursued by demons of his own making. What had he seen and done in seeking vengeance for his wife's murder?

In the few days that Manny had known J.T., he had come to like him—but he knew that he would never be like him. When he had fired the pistol at the men from the gang, he had aimed as well as he could, but it wasn't just lack of experience with the weapon that had caused him to miss. He knew, now, that he just wasn't a killer. And J.T. was.

The trail gradually wound through light woodland that eventually gave way to open plain. There were occasional signs of human occupation; a sign pointing to a farm too far off the trail to be seen, or the start of a fence along the side of a field. Manny realised that he now owned some land. What would he do with it? He had heard his father and uncle talk late into the nights during the long journey, making plans for the new Nussbaum farm. He remembered some of what they had said, but he had no idea how he might make any of it happen. His parents had lived on the plains of eastern Europe and worked on other people's farms. The dream to have their own had brought, or perhaps driven, them to America. Manny had been born in New York, though, and knew nothing about farming. He could, perhaps, sell the land...but then what?

Manny had seen enough small towns on his way through Kansas to know how small they could be. Madison Springs was bigger than some. The trail took them over a rise, from the top of which they could see the whole town laid out. Manny estimated about forty buildings with plenty of space between them.

"We'll make a report to the sheriff first," said J.T. "My friend is staying in a room at the saloon. We should be able to get some food there."

J.T. was leading them to the mid-point of the main street. "Joan told me that the sheriff's office was just down there to the right, but there's a good chance he won't be there," said J.T. "If he's good at his job, he'll be out doing it. If he's not, he may be still home, or in the saloon."

J.T. led them in the opposite direction from the sheriff's office.

"First things first."

Silence brought them to a halt outside a livery yard. He dismounted and gestured for Manny to do the same, and then called into the open yard of the livery. A boy, just a bit younger than Manny, came out and J.T. gave him a couple of coins for watering and seeing to the horse and pony for the next couple of hours.

"Look after your horse first and they'll be ready when you most need them," J.T. said. "I often find, when I ride into a town holding a rifle in my hand that the sheriff finds me before I waste my time looking for him." He nodded toward an overweight figure walking up the street toward them. A lawman's badge was clearly visible on the man's shirt. "Be sure to give him the best description of Carlson that you can."

The sheriff gave a friendly smile as he greeted them. "Good day to you folks. Welcome to Madison Springs." He was perspiring freely and took off his hat and waved it in front of his face to cool himself down. "I'm Sheriff Bolton. Can I help you with your business today?"

Manny saw Bolton look at the rifle that J.T. carried loosely in his hand.

"I'm just passing through," J.T. said. "I found this boy a day's ride east of here. His family members were all killed in an attack on their wagons. Same bunch of raiders attacked Joan Adams's farm. Four men. I can describe three of them, and the boy, here, can give you a good description of the other one. Thought you would want to know they were in your area."

"And how right you are," the sheriff replied. "I'm real sorry about your family, son." He gave what looked to Manny like a genuine smile. "Let's get to my office and write this all up, official like." He shook his head from side to side as they walked along. "Terrible, terrible."

The sheriff's office was cramped once all three of them were inside. Manny could see that the rear room was equipped with a couple of bunks and a lock hanging loose on the door. No one seemed to be in there.

"Are you sure that the same group made both raids?" Bolton asked J.T. while he dug in a desk drawer for something to write on.

"You think you might have two groups of gunmen riding around your county?" said Silence. He went on to describe the events at the farm and the features of the three men he'd seen before asking Manny to describe Carlson.

"And you say this Carlson had been your family's guide all the way from St. Louis?" Bolton asked Manny directly. "He may be on his way back there, but I'll put the word out and we'll see if we can't find these men for you." Again, he smiled warmly at Manny.

****

Silence led Manny to the saloon and asked the owner if

Captain Hawton was around. A girl was sent out to see if Hawton was available. J.T. ordered soup and bread for the two of them and the owner showed them to a table.

"I don't want to disappoint you, Manny, but our chat with the sheriff didn't go how I had hoped it would."

"He didn't ask any of the questions I would have asked," Manny said, sighing. "He didn't ask if they took anything or where we were travelling to. He didn't even ask you if you saw which direction they went after they left the farm."

"You're a clever boy, Manny," said J.T. "You deserve better than all this."

"We all deserve better," a new voice insisted. Manny looked up to see a man in a chair on wheels being pushed toward their table by the saloon girl.

"Good to see you again, J.T., and glad to see you brought a friend."

"Captain Hawton," said J.T. acknowledging the greeting. "This is Manny Nussbaum."

"Pleased to meet you, Mr. Nussbaum," the captain said.

The use of the title which Manny still felt applied to his father jolted him. The man in the chair smiled at him in what he felt sure was supposed to be a reassuring way. He was less genial than the sheriff had been, but seemed more genuine in comparison.

"Sally," the captain said, turning to the girl, "could you bring us all some coffee?"

The girl went off to the back room to start some fresh coffee. With no further small talk, J.T. started relating the events of the attacks on Manny's family and Joan's farm to Captain Hawton. The captain listened attentively and interjected now and then with questions.

"I'm afraid J.T. is right in his lack of faith in the sheriff, here," said Hawton when Silence was done with the account. "Bolton does a fair job of keeping the drunks off the street in town, but rarely ventures beyond the limits. However, I have some contacts of my own which I might be able to use to find out more about that gang."

The saloon keeper arrived with a pot of coffee and some mugs.

Once the saloon keeper had gone, J.T. suggested it was odd that the girl had not brought the coffee, and perhaps Manny might like to keep an eye out for her while he was looking in on the horses. It was silently acknowledged between them that J.T. wanted to talk to Captain Hawton privately, and Manny took the hint easily.

Captain Hawton pulled a closed envelope out of his jacket pocket and held it close to his chest. "I sent a message because I have news about Brady. You'll make me happy if you tell me to burn it."

"Sorry, Captain," said Silence. "This will be the end, I promise, but I need to close this once and for all."

"You've tracked down all the killers, J.T., and Brady wasn't even there."

"He should've been. I hired him to manage the farm while I was away. I'll give him a chance to explain why he left my family open to attack by raiders, but he'll need to be persuasive."

****

Manny left the saloon quickly enough to see the saloon girl talking to a man at the far end of the street. He could see that the man was wearing a brown hat, but could make out few other details without getting closer. Trying not to be noticed, he sauntered over to look in on the livery yard to see that the lad there was carefully rubbing down the horse while the pony was feeding. Satisfied, he wandered around the small town. He saw the girl, Sally, from the saloon walking toward the saloon rather than away from it. She saw him and crossed the street to talk to him.

"You must be someone special, to be keeping company with the captain and his army friend," the girl said, only half teasingly.

Manny shrugged, unsure of the response the girl was expecting.

"My name's Sally."

"I'm Manny."

"What an interesting name. You're not Mormon, are you?"

"No." Manny hadn't been told by J.T. not to give out personal information too readily, but it seemed a good idea not to be too free with details given the restrained response from the sheriff. Manny pointed in the direction Sally had just walked from. "I'm looking around while J.T talks to the captain. Is there much that way?"

"Only more houses and the general store. Oh, and the chapel, too, which they use as a school weekdays."

"I'll go and look in the store for a bit." Manny said thanks and good bye to Sally, and walked along the street while she hurried back to the saloon. He could no longer see the man she had been talking to but had made a mental note of the building they had been standing by. When he reached it, this turned out to be the store Sally had mentioned.

The town's only general store had a deck around the front and one side. There was a single step up to the door. Manny entered and looked around. There were two other customers, one of which was wearing a brown hat and, Manny now saw, a gun belt. The gun belt was not empty.

The other customer was a heavy set woman who was chatting to the storekeeper about a range of subjects. Manny went to the opposite end of the store from the man with the gun. He had a few coins on him and looked for something he could get for Joan and Cassie. He found a couple of buttons which looked a close match to the ones Cassie had lost in the attack. She'd not been able to find them when she had gone back to the stream later. He was less sure what to buy for Joan, but found some ribbons that his mother would have liked, and hoped Joan didn't have dissimilar tastes.

As he went to the counter to pay, he saw that the man in the brown hat was standing by the shelves stocking tobacco. He seemed to be trying to look at Manny without being noticed, which suited Manny, who had feared some kind of ugly confrontation which he could only come out worse in.

Manny paid for the gifts and managed to avoid getting drawn into a conversation with the storekeeper who was still discussing the prospects of rain with the woman customer, even though she had long since paid for her own supplies.

Walking back, Manny decided to go by the blacksmith's which

allowed him to cross the street in a way that he could glance round to see if the gunman had come out of the store to watch or follow him. He saw that the man had, indeed, come out after him, but had claimed one of the horses from the front of the general store and was riding out of town at what seemed a fair pace to a novice rider such as Manny.

****

J.T. and the Captain listened as Manny recounted his observations of the girl and the man with the gun.

"Your presence has been noted, J.T.," Captain Hawton said quietly. "Another reason why it might be best not to proceed with this business of yours."

Manny looked at J.T. and wondered what business the captain was referring to. J.T. changed the subject.

"I've been asking the captain, here, what to do about your family's land. It should rightfully belong to you, but you'll need to make a proper claim. If you don't, it'll revert to the Territory, and probably be sold again. The circuit judge for this area only comes to town a couple of days every few months, and is next due in six days' time. I think I'll get you back to Joan's, and you can come into town again when the judge gets here."

"The judge is a fair man, although he doesn't look like one," Captain Hawton chipped in. "He's certainly your best bet for getting your land, and he may be able to do more than this sheriff about the scum that killed your family."

Chapter Six

Manny rode quietly in line behind J.T.'s horse as they left the town behind them. The man in front was even more taciturn than usual, and Manny's one attempt to ask after J.T.'s plans had been met with a "not yet". As they left the cleared land around Madison Springs and started riding into the patchy woodland, Silence spoke.

"Come and ride alongside me, Manny."

Manny nudged his pony forward until they were riding side by side. J.T. was some way up still with the combined extra height of his horse against the pony added to his natural height advantage over the boy. Manny saw that J.T. was trying to lean slowly closer.

"Do you think you can remember the way back to the farm from here?" J.T. asked.

Manny nodded. There had not been so many junctions in the path on the way here that he thought he couldn't work it out.

"Reach into my saddlebag and take out the pistol," J.T. said, softly. "I think we may have company up ahead. I can get off one shot with this rifle if I need to, but I can't aim too well or reload with this damn shoulder. If there is trouble, fire off a shot or two in the general direction of any gunfire, and then ride for the farm as quickly as you can."

Manny looked at J.T with concern.

"Don't worry," J.T said, dropping the level of his voice still further. "There are tracks of one horse having come along ahead of us not too long ago. Whoever it was rode off the path about fifty yards back and is probably watching us from the clump of trees over to the left—*no, don't look.* If they wanted to shoot at us, they would probably have done so by now. Someone seems very curious about one or other of us."

"Or both of us," Manny said.

"It's possible. I wonder…"

They rode on in silence until the trees on the left gave way to a rough meadow. When they reached a place where the hay had grown tall, J.T. slowed to a halt and signalled Manny to bring his pony to a standstill.

"I want you to keep riding. I'm going to circle back and see if I can get a look at our friend back there."

Manny nodded in agreement and urged the pony forward again. He looked back after only a minute or so, but J.T. was already out of sight. He felt very alone among the tall grasses and bushes that seemed to crowd in on him from the side of the trail. He tried to think about getting back to Joan and Cassie, but found only pictures of his mother and father and sister flooding his memory. He leant forward to pat the pony on the neck, grateful for this companion, at least.

****

J.T. looked along the barrel of his rifle at the man in the brown hat. It was a simple shot, if he wanted to make it. The man was standing by his horse, drinking from a canteen of water. His back was toward J.T. and he seemed oblivious to the fact that he was under observation. Silence had tracked many people over the last few years, and they only knew he was there if he wanted them to. He was happy for this man to go away thinking he had completed his task undetected.

The man in the brown hat mounted his horse and rode back in the direction of Madison Springs. J.T. smiled thinly and lowered his rifle. He'd know the man again if he saw him.

****

Manny was half-lost in memories of family life back in New York when he heard what sounded like a horse behind him. The sounds of the animal were still enough of a novelty to the city-born boy that he could pick them out amid the rapid onset of the evening darkness. He thought quickly about his options. He was fairly sure that the farm was about half-a-mile ahead. The pony had been walking the whole way, and might have it in her to run the rest of the way, although Manny was less than sure that he could stay on the pony at any great pace.

He could ride off the trail and try and hide, but couldn't really see how to cover the tracks of the pony. He slowed to a halt and reached down for the pistol that J.T. had given him. He listened intently to the sounds of the horses' hooves on the path—at first, barely audible, but gradually louder. When he thought the distance between himself and the rider was about right, he called out.

"Who's there? I have a gun."

"I know. I gave it to you and I never intended for you to use it to shoot my horse—which is where you're aiming, at the moment."

Manny noticed that the gun had already dropped so he was aiming at a downward angle because he still lacked the strength to hold the gun steady, but he was pleased to recognise J.T.'s voice.

"I'm glad it's you, Mr. Silence," Manny said. He could now see J.T. clearly.

****

Joan saw J.T. and Manny were supplied with apple pie and fresh coffee on their return. Cassie and Joan joined them around the table. After reassuring them that his shoulder was feeling stronger, J.T. proceeded to eat quietly.

"Well?" Joan asked. "What devil's trail is old Hawton sending you on this time?"

"It's Brady," J.T. replied. "The captain told me Brady is working for a man called Frank Decker at a ranch just west of here."

Joan let out a slow whistle. "Now, that's another reason just to let this all go, J.T., aside from the fact that enough is long since enough. Frank Decker has a ranch alright; a mighty big one, and a whole lot of men working for him. If Decker is protecting Brady, you won't get near him."

Silence said nothing.

Silence Rides Alone

****

Manny was returning to the house from emptying the water from washing the dishes when he saw the silhouette on the porch. It was J.T., and Manny sensed he was waiting to speak to him.

There were a few insects flying about, but otherwise, it was a pleasantly cool evening after the heat of the day. Manny sat down on a bench which was set at an angle; half-facing out into the darkness and half-facing toward J.T. Silence.

"I've spoken to Joan, but I want to talk to you, as well—about what happens next," J.T. said. "I've got to go over and see if I can talk to Brady; the man you heard me talk about earlier. When that's done, I'll come back here and take you into town again so that you can see the judge about your family's land. Have you thought about what you'll do if he backs your claim?"

"I know I don't want to go back to New York, but I also know I can't turn a piece of land into a farm on my own."

"I've a feeling it may not be the type of land best suited to planting crops. You might do better with livestock—but that'll cost more money than you have."

Which is nothing, thought Manny.

"You could sell the land," said J.T. "I was going to ask Joan if you could stay with her and Cassie, but she was too quick and suggested it first. They can use an extra hand, as I'm sure you've worked out by now. Especially one that'll grow bigger and stronger, courtesy of Joan's cooking. No one's trying to replace your family, but Joan and Cassie are about as good as it gets."

"You could stay, too," Manny said.

Silence shook his head. "Maybe one day, but not yet."

Chapter Seven

J.T. Silence kept his horse at walking pace as he approached the Decker ranch. An open gateway marked the start of the home farm area, but Silence suspected that much of the land he had been riding through for the last hour or so also belonged to the same ranch. He'd decided on a straightforward visit and enquiry to Decker about Brady, at least in the first instance.

The man just inside the farm boundary wore a gun and made no pretence at being anything other than a guard. Many ranches expected their hired hands to be able to defend themselves, and sometimes more, but to have someone on the payroll who did no actual ranch work struck Silence as odd.

Silence rode straight toward the man and nodded to acknowledge his presence.

"I've come to pay my respects to Mr. Decker," J.T. said.

"Tether your horse by the fence, there, and follow me."

The man turned his back on Silence and walked toward the largest of several buildings. This was a two-story house of recent construction. There was also a stable and a one-story building that he assumed was a bunk house. A large barn and a couple of sheds stood slightly farther off.

The farm itself looked busy enough. A couple of hands were in a paddock trying to break in a young horse. Another horse, this one full grown, was having its shoes replaced. J.T. followed his guide up to the main house where he was told to wait while the man went inside.

J.T. noticed one man who was neither working nor looking like he intended to. He wore a clean white shirt, and was leaning against the wall of the bunk house and smoking. Silence had not seen him before, but recognised the type. The man had the look of someone hired to use a gun rather than a shovel. His eyes had already met Silence's and he tipped his hat, almost imperceptibly. The gunfighter raised a hand to take the cigarette from his mouth and he smiled thinly at Silence. He was around thirty years of age, with an appearance suggesting he was not a novice at his chosen trade.

J.T. was led into a side door to the main house. The room he was in was a single-story annex to the main building, and clearly served as some kind of office. At one end was an imposing desk behind which sat the second man J.T. had seen this morning who didn't seem like he was looking to do any farm work anytime soon.

In this case, the figure exuded both authority and comfort. The only other person in the room was a girl of around nineteen. She was pouring coffee. Standing up, the man reached across his desk to offer Silence his hand.

"Good morning. I'm Frank Decker. Would you like some coffee? My daughter just brewed it."

Silence nodded in thanks to the girl and said "Thank you, miss."

The girl took an extra cup from a sideboard and poured a small coffee which she handed to Silence. She then turned to her father. "I'll leave you to it, Papa. Don't work too late." She opened an internal door which Silence rightly assumed led to the rest of the house. She smiled at him as she pulled the door closed behind her.

"I'm told you wanted to see me. If it's about a job, I still got a couple of spots for the right type of man."

"Thank you," replied J.T. "I'm not looking for work right now. I'm looking for a man I heard might be working here. Name of Brady."

"Sorry, Mr. ah..." Decker said.

"Silence."

J.T. spotted a flicker of recognition on Decker's face as he gave his name.

"Well, I'm sorry, Mr. Silence, but I've got no hands working for me by that name. I did hear that some of the farms south of here take on casual labour this time of year. You could try them."

"Thanks for your time, Mr. Decker," J.T. said. "I'll do that."

"Well, fine. I wish you luck, and if you change your mind about a job, come back and see me."

Decker rose from his seat to show Silence out. Once outside, he waved to a couple of men to come over. One of them was the hired gun Silence had seen earlier. The other was the man in the brown hat who had followed J.T. and Manny out of Madison Springs.

"These boys are riding into town for the night," Decker said. "You may as well ride with them. Sheriff told me there's been a gang causing trouble in the area. Shot some poor family in their wagons, apparently. I'm sure you know how to handle yourself, but safety in numbers, eh?"

"Thanks again," J.T. said. He was disinclined to ride alongside any of Decker's men, but if there was going to be trouble, he'd rather it was away from the farm where there was just the two men than here where he was heavily outnumbered.

****

The evening crickets were beginning to make their presence heard as the three men rode the rough trail back to Madison Springs. The conversations had been minimal, so far.

Silence had learned that the man in the brown hat was called Roberts, and his more dangerous-looking colleague gave his name as Van Hook.

On the basis of his ride out here, he reckoned on another hour before they reached town, and it would be dark before then. He was about to tell the two men that he needed to ride on quicker if he was to reach town and still have time to get back to Joan's farm, when he heard sounds off to the left that were not made by crickets or other wildlife.

Silence saw that one of his companions, the gunman, Van Hook, had also noticed the noise. He gestured to Roberts to slow to a halt. Both Silence and Van Hook quietly slipped out of their saddles, took their rifles and crept through the shrubs toward the sounds of the noise. Silence noticed that, like himself, Van Hook was walking at an angle, almost crab like, to avoid the noise his legs would make brushing past each other if they crossed.

Silence could see signs of a campfire ahead of them. There were also the voices of several men talking. Van Hook leaned close enough to whisper to him.

"Could be the gang that's been causing trouble. You want to take a closer look?"

Silence nodded. Roberts, having tied the horses to a tree, had caught up with them, and Van Hook indicated for him to circle round to one side.

That they managed to get close enough to the group of men for Silence to positively identify them as the ones who had attacked Joan and Cassie, and presumably also Manny's family, Silence put down to the quantity of liquor the outlaws appeared to be consuming. He turned to Van Hook and nodded to indicate they were the men in question. Van Hook motioned to Silence in a manner suggesting it was his call what they did next.

Silence thought quickly. If they left quietly now and reported to the sheriff, Silence had little confidence that he would come out until the next day when the gang could be long gone. As they were now, they might be outnumbered—but only by four to three. They had the element of surprise, and Silence felt sure that his companions knew how to use their guns—while their opponents were all at least partly the worse for drink.

He mouthed silently to Van Hook, "Alive". Van Hook shrugged as if to say he didn't mind whether he killed four men or not.

Silence led the way. He emerged into the clearing where the gang were camping with his rifle aimed at the men. He saw briefly a look of surprise on the four men's faces when he felt a mighty thud against the back of his head. He felt another impact as he hit the ground, and then nothing.

Chapter Eight

J.T. Silence woke suddenly, but without moving. He had trained himself to be able to wake and use his sense to know what was going on around him before he moved and gave himself away to anyone who might be hostile. What his senses told him quickly were that he had a pain in the back of his head where he had been hit, presumably by Van Hook. He had a taste of cheap whisky in his mouth. Opening his eyes, he could see the ground immediately beneath him and could also tell that it was daylight and he'd therefore been unconscious right through the night. His sense of smell told him that someone was smoking tobacco nearby, and his hearing told him that at least one pair of boots was walking softly close by. He also heard a voice.

"Good morning. I can see you're stirring. You might want to get up now."

Silence pushed himself up to a squatting position and took in the scene around him. It didn't look pleasant. Sheriff Bolton was standing next to two horses, one of which was Silence's. He was smoking while covering Silence with a pistol. Just beyond Bolton were four bodies. The ground under and around each of them was an almost ebon, crimson colour from spilled and long congealed blood. It was the four members of the gang that he'd come across with Van Hook and Roberts, of whom there was no sign now. Silence, beginning to guess what had happened, was not surprised at the absence of his temporary companions.

"Dead," said Bolton. "Three of 'em shot in the back. I figured you for a better man than that, although I'll give you credit for your tracking abilities to surprise a group that size."

"I didn't kill them," Silence said as he slowly stood up.

"Someone knocked me unconscious before this happened." His face showed distaste as he gestured at the bodies.

"Sure, and this isn't your Henry rifle and spent shells, here."

"It's mine, but any man west of the Mississippi knows how to use one of those."

"Well, from where I'm standing I see four men dead and one man living and the man living owns the gun that killed the four corpses," Bolton said. "Could be you killed those men, then drank yourself to sleep." He kicked a couple of empty whisky bottles. "There's enough whisky been drunk here to put you and your horse out for the count. Now, you get up on your horse, there, and you can tell me your story on the way back to town. I'll send my deputy out with a cart to collect the bodies."

Bolton kept a gun aimed at Silence while they both mounted the their horses. The sheriff also insisted that Silence ride a little ahead of him so he could keep him covered on the way back. The sheriff listened to Silence's version of events without comment until the end.

"So, you're telling me that those four men are the gang that killed the family of that boy you helped and also attacked two women friends of yours," Bolton said. "Looks to me like you're admitting a motive as well as being on the spot at the time of the killings. Still, if these men Van Hook and Roberts can confirm your story, then you'll be clear. If not, well the dead men weren't exactly saints, so I doubt a jury will be too hard on you."

Silence kept quiet rather than point out that if he hadn't killed the men then it must have been Van Hook and Roberts—who were hardly likely to admit to it.

The rest of the journey back to Madison Springs passed without conversation. The sheriff seemed uninterested in talking, and Silence was mulling over events and trying to piece things together.

On their arrival back in town, Bolton took his prisoner directly to the jail and ordered Silence to sit on the bench bed in the back room while he was locked in.

"Can I send a message to someone?" Silence asked as the sheriff took the key out of the lock and hooked it onto his belt.

"I can probably arrange that."

The sheriff passed Silence a small pad and stubby pencil. Silence wrote a short note for Captain Hawton saying little more than where he was and that he was accused of killing four men. He told Bolton that Hawton could be found at the saloon.

Once the sheriff had gone off, Silence looked around the cell. Apart from the bunk and a bucket in the corner, for the necessary, there was only a pack of cards. Silence counted them. Forty-nine cards but five aces. About what he expected from this sheriff. He lay on the bed and closed his eyes.

****

A tin canteen rattling on the bars woke Silence from his light sleep.

"Visitor for you," Bolton called out.

Silence looked up, but where he had expected to see Captain Hawton wheeling himself into the room, it was Cassie and Manny who were being shown through the front room of the sheriff's office. Bolton passed them a three legged stool for one of them to sit on, but conspicuously kept his chair and sat down himself within earshot of any conversation that might pass between Silence and his visitors.

In response to the initial question from Cassie of what had happened to him, Silence told his story again just as he had told it to Sheriff Bolton. He added no new information, nor any of his deductions. What he did do was to look Cassie straight in the eye whenever he reached part of his account which he wanted her to be sure was significant. *Decker denied Brady worked for him. Van Hook and Roberts had accompanied him when he had found the gang, but had been absent in the morning. The sheriff had already arrived when Silence came to after being knocked out.* Bolton, who was looking elsewhere in his act of not listening in to the conversation, missed all this.

"I was expecting to see Captain Hawton when I heard I had a visitor," Silence said.

"We were with him when he got your message." Cassie said. "When you didn't return to the farm last night, we decide to ride in to town with the sunrise to see if anything was wrong."

Silence looked around the locked cell. "What could possibly be wrong?"

Manny smiled at the joke, but Cassie frowned at Silence.

"Given that Captain Hawton usually seems to know more than is good for anyone about what goes on, we went to see him first. We had only been there five minutes when your note arrived. The saloon girl, Sally, brought it in."

"Did Joan come in to town with you?" Silence asked.

"She stayed home," Cassie replied.

"Louis is with her," Manny chipped in.

"But I'm not too happy about leaving her alone. I don't like to leave you here, J.T., but I think we need to be riding home soon. Your horse is being looked after by the blacksmith's lad. We'll go and let the captain know you're well. The judge is due in town the day after tomorrow. Maybe we can get everything sorted out then. How is the shoulder?"

"Nearly back to normal."

"Look after yourself, J.T."

"As best as I can. Thanks for coming Cassie."

"The lad, here, threatened to come even if we tried to stop him," Cassie said.

Silence nodded in thanks to Manny.

****

Captain Hawton had already wheeled himself out into the open air in front of the saloon when Cassie and Manny reached him. Manny offered to help push the chair.

"Very kind of you, sir," Hawton said.

Cassie noticed how pleased Manny looked at being addressed as 'sir'. She could see how Hawton had gained a reputation for being an army officer whose men would follow him anywhere. It was widely known that he had an ongoing role in the army despite the injury which had reduced him to the chair.

Officially, that seemed to be the job of buying cattle to be taken for beef for the forts further west. Most people accepted that, but Cassie suspected that his travels around the Territory were also used for other matters.

"I think a little turn around town will do me the power of good," Hawton said as Manny pushed the chair along the side of the street. At a whisper, Hawton added, "And getting away from other ears may not be a bad idea, either."

Manny noticed Sally had been sitting on the step of the saloon peeling potatoes. He saw that she had noticed him looking in her direction and was smiling at him. He smiled, but then turned back to concentrate on handling the wheelchair.

Once they were out of earshot of anyone else, Cassie started telling Captain Hawton what had happened to Silence. She explained the points that Silence had seemed to be stressing were important.

"So, if we piece things together, what do we have?" Hawton asked, and then continued before anyone else could attempt an answer. "J.T. had gone out to Decker's ranch to ask about a man called Brady, who I know for a fact has been working for Decker, yet Decker denies any knowledge of the man."

"Which tells us that Decker is lying...but why?" Cassie asked. "The business between Silence and Brady is from years back, and I can't believe Brady is anything but another hired hand to Frank Decker."

"Maybe we're looking at things from the wrong angle," replied Hawton. "We also know that the two men who started riding back to town with J.T. were working for Decker. I've seen Roberts around town several times in the week or so I've been here. Also, Manny's seen him with Sally from the saloon. I've never met Van Hook, but I've heard his name. I doubt if either one was hired by Decker for their skills in putting up fences or breaking horses. Van Hook, in particular, has a reputation which suggests he is dangerous.

"Clearly, Van Hook knocked Silence unconscious, and we can also presume that he killed the four men."

"No great loss," said Cassie.

"Perhaps not, but if Van Hook and Roberts did kill them, what was their purpose? If they were trying to help rid the area of outlaws, why not work with Silence to do just that?"

"They've succeeded in getting Silence in jail," suggested Manny.

"True," said Hawton. "Normally, I'd say he stood little chance of being found guilty of anything other than ridding the area of a menace, but I've a nasty feeling about the make-up of the jury he may have. My fears arise from the presence of Sheriff Bolton at the scene before Silence was even conscious. Given that Bolton is known for not leaving town that often, it seems somewhat suspicious that he was on the spot at just the wrong time for J.T. He could only know where to go from either Van Hook or Roberts."

"I never thought that much of Bolton," said Cassie "but I never thought of him as crooked."

"Like a lot of small towns, this one doesn't pay its sheriff much," said Hawton. "If someone offers him a little extra, he'd be in company with a lot of others if he was tempted."

"Someone like Frank Decker, you mean," Cassie said.

"We also need to take into consideration that if Decker is willing and able to buy off the sheriff, then he could probably do the same with enough of a jury for J.T. to be in real danger of swinging for the deaths of those four."

They had walked as far as the blacksmith while they had been talking. At the same time, a cart driven by the deputy had arrived in front of the small hardware store that also doubled as an undertaker's establishment. The sides of the cart were not high and it was easy to see, even from a little way off, that the cart bore human bodies.

"If you need to go and make sure, we'll understand," Hawton said to Manny.

"Thank you. I think I should." The youth walked the short distance to the cart, which was already attracting attention from other townsfolk curious to see the faces of the gang they had heard about. The deputy had been thoughtful enough to place the bodies face up in order to avoid anyone seeing the unholy messes that had been their backs until someone shot into them from close distance. The fronts of their torsos would have been as bad, but for strategically placed blankets.

Manny looked at the four faces. Three, he recognised clearly from the shoot-out at Joan and Cassie's farm. The fourth, he knew even better. It was Carlson. He'd never really doubted that the same gang that killed his family had also attacked them at the farm, but the proof that lay in front of him made his mouth go dry.

Cassie had come over to stand beside him. She put her arm around him and spoke quietly.

"It won't bring them back, Manny, but maybe they can rest easier now."

"I thought I'd feel more satisfaction from knowing the men who killed my family are dead."

"It's to your credit that you don't," Cassie said. "That's the difference between you and those men."

"And what about J.T.? Is he like me—or like them?"

"J.T. is a third type. I know he hates doing some of the things he has done even though he feels he has to do them. I wish he hadn't chosen the life he's led in recent years, but at the same time, I don't think he has done anything just to make himself feel good."

Manny and Cassie made their way back through the growing crowd that had gathered to gawk at the dead bodies. They found the captain on the opposite side of the street.

"Doesn't look like there is a lot of love for those men in this town," Hawton said.

"In which case, if Decker had his hired guns kill them, why not take the credit?" asked Cassie. "I've heard he's in with the political groups. He could win himself a lot of votes on a law and order ticket."

"Even if it's vigilante action?"

"It's happened before," Cassie observed.

"So, we have to ask ourselves what he gains by framing J.T. and by killing those men that would be worth more to him than some extra popularity with the voters."

"You have a theory, I take it," Cassie said.

Captain Hawton looked around to see if anyone was close by. Nobody was. Anyone who was able to leave homes or work was across the street finding out about the dead men.

"I think those men were working for Decker. I think he had them killed to keep them from talking. Given that we know they attacked your family, Manny, and your farm, Cassie—without trying to take anything much in either case—it seems likely that he is trying to get rid of you. But, I don't yet know why—and unfortunately, I can't prove any of that."

"But I'm betting you have more of an idea than we do," Cassie said.

"Well, I've had an eye on Mr. Decker for a while," said Hawton. "He's been recruiting some none-too-savoury types to work at his ranch. Brady, Roberts and Van Hook are three, but there are others up there, as well. He must have money to spend as Van Hook, in particular, demands a high wage." Hawton politely asked Manny to turn the wheel chair around as they had reached the end of the street. "I also know that he has links to one of the political groups that is angling to get power after the Territory gets statehood."

Cassie looked back up the main street whose length they had just walked. "Look! Is that who I think it is with the sheriff?"

"I recognise Roberts, so I think we can assume the other man is Van Hook," replied Hawton.

The three men they could see from a distance disappeared into the sheriff's office.

****

Silence was awake and alert to see his new visitors arrive. The sheriff called out all the same.

"More visitors, Silence." The sheriff brought Van Hook and Roberts through so that they could see the solitary man in the basic cell.

"These here gentlemen are Mr. Van Hook and Mr. Roberts," Sheriff Bolton addressed Silence. "I brought them here to see if they can vouch for your story about last night."

"Sorry sheriff, I've never seen this man before," said Van Hook. He shrugged nonchalantly, took a tin of tobacco out of his jacket pocket and started putting together a cigarette.

"Me either," said Roberts.

Silence had expected the denials, and kept his face impassive. The sheriff, however, made a point of looking sympathetic.

"Well, that's a real shame, boys," Bolton said. "Thank you, all the same." The two gunmen walked casually out of the small office.

Bolton turned toward his prisoner. "Looks like you're going to have to see what the judge and jury make of your story, Silence. I guess that's how it should be in any case. All democratic and legal-like."

Silence said nothing but looked directly into Sheriff Bolton's eyes. The piercing look from his steely blue eyes said more than any words. The sheriff coughed artificially as a way of breaking off eye contact and made his excuses, leaving J.T. Silence once more to the quiet of the cell.

J.T. was about to settle back into his half sleep when he heard the door open yet again. It was not the sheriff returning, but Van Hook. The killer walked over to Bolton's desk and picked up the tin of tobacco he had deliberately left lying there earlier. He looked over at Silence and smiled thinly.

"Tonight, midnight," Van Hook said, and then left straightaway.

Chapter Nine

Manny had listened quietly while Cassie had given her account of the day's events to Joan over the evening meal. Joan had tutted at several points but generally listened without comment until Cassie had finished.

"It's not good, but I can see a little more light than old Captain Hawton," Joan said, after a lingering few moments when nobody had said anything. "He doesn't know the people of this town as well as he thinks if he believes Frank Decker can buy a whole jury. There are folks who are good and honest, no matter what. There are also those that have no love for Decker as a result of his business practices. Add to that the fact that few people will be anything other than pleased that those four outlaws are dead, and I believe J.T. will be safe from the noose.

"What does give me pause for thought, though, is that Decker is no fool. He must know he could never buy a whole jury either, so why go to all this trouble to keep J.T. in jail for what is likely to be only a few days?"

"What would Mr. Silence be doing if he was free in those days?" asked Manny.

"Now, that is a good question to ask," Joan said.

"He'd be looking for Brady and maybe staying here with us some of the time," Cassie said.

"Which means that Decker may be anxious to see one or other of those things doesn't happen," Joan mused.

"Or both," said Manny.

Nothing more was said, but they all knew the significance. If Decker wanted to make sure that Silence was not here at the farm, it was to be certain he was not able to protect two women and a boy. The implication was chilling.

****

Captain Hawton checked the barrels of his revolver before setting it to rest under the blanket he kept over his lap. He looked around the small room he'd rented in the saloon. It had been the only one available on the ground floor, and he preferred not to put himself in a position where he couldn't get out on his own if he needed to. He allowed other people to push the wheelchair for him, but he could do ably when required.

The room had one exit he could use, which was the single door. There was also a window that was low enough to the floor that he could pull himself through it using the strength in his arms. He'd tested this idea earlier, and while the effort had been immense, he had got far enough to know he could escape that way if necessary. He did not expect that he would come under any direct attack, but the possibility was there. There was certainly something in the wind that evening which the captain sensed.

Captain Hawton lived on a half-pension from the army which he had served for many years prior to the accident that had robbed him of the use of his legs. In return, he toured towns and farms buying up beef and fodder for the cavalry based farther west.

Beyond that, his status was vague, even to himself. He had no written contract with anyone but maintained routes of communication that reached back to Washington. He was, as Silence knew and Cassie suspected, an intelligence agent. As such, he hid in plain sight. Everyone knew he worked for the army and was well-connected. He was protected by the knowledge that his death would be avenged by the powers of the U.S. Army. That left him vulnerable only to those too stupid to realise that certainty.

Decker did not come into the stupid category, but some of his men might. Hawton patted the revolver again as he snuffed out the single candle in his room. Unfortunately, he thought, the protection that he enjoyed did not reach out to cover the likes of J.T. Silence, the two women, or the boy.

****

Silence flicked another playing card through the darkness of his cell to hit the lock a few feet away. The quiet rattle from the impact would have told him he had been accurate yet again if his eyes had not already adjusted to the dark sufficiently for him to see quite well the area around him. The sheriff had locked the outer office door some hours earlier after having let Sally from the saloon in with a covered meal that Captain Hawton had arranged to be sent over. The girl had been wearing a tighter than usual blouse and been most friendly to the sheriff. After she'd set down the tray next to Silence's bed, she'd hung around long enough to ask the sheriff whether she would be seeing him over at the saloon later. Bolton had told her he'd be over once he'd seen his prisoner was set for the night.

Silence had no pocket watch, but thought it must be an hour or two yet to midnight. The not very subtle luring away of the sheriff and the cryptic comment from Van Hook meant something would happen. He flicked another playing card and hit the lock again.

****

Manny woke up at the first bark from Louis. The dog had been allowed to sleep at the foot of the bed that Manny had been using at the farm. It was the most comfortable bed that Manny had ever known, although the competition was the cramped bunk he had shared with his cousin in New York and the sleeping roll under the wagon on the journey west. Despite the comparative comfort, Manny was instantly awake.

Louis had jumped off the bed and was barking at the door and wall. The dog was clearly alert to some perceived danger outside. Manny trusted the dog's instincts and opened the door but only after he made sure he had a hold on Louis. He didn't want to lose this final friend and link to his family.

Joan and Cassie emerged from their own rooms, also alerted by the barking of the dog. They were both in the process of throwing coats over their night wear as they made for the front door to the farm house.

As soon as they all stepped outside, the danger was clear. The barn had been set alight. The flames were not yet wild, but given how dry everything was, it would not take long.

"The horses!" shouted Joan as she ran toward the barn. Cassie followed her, and Manny was about to do the same when he was pulled to one side by Louis. The dog was trying to get away so that he could chase what Manny now saw was the silhouette of a man riding a horse at full gallop through the night. Manny caught up with Cassie and pointed out the rider to her.

"Let him go," Cassie said. "The animals come first."

****

Silence heard the key in the lock of the outside door and recognised Roberts as the visitor, even in the darkness. He was carrying a large canteen under his arm.

"I'm here to get you out," Roberts said.

"Why should I leave?" Silence replied. "I'm innocent of killing those men, as you, I suspect, know full well. You could have helped me out of here a lot easier by telling the truth to the sheriff this afternoon if you were concerned about my welfare."

Roberts started unscrewing the lid to the canteen. He tipped it up and started emptying liquid over the sheriff's desk. Once that was done, he emptied the remaining contents around the rest of the room. He took the time to shake some through into the back room which was Silence's cell.

Silence felt some of the liquid land on his trousers. He put his finger on it and brought it up to his nose. *Kerosene. Flammable.*

"I'm also here to burn this little building to the ground, so stay if you want, but I think you'll want to come with me."

Roberts chose another key from the chain that Silence recognised as the one that Bolton usually wore. He wondered if the sheriff had handed them over or whether they had been obtained in some more sinister way. The door to the cell was unlocked and Roberts gestured for Silence to come out slowly.

"Keep in front of me the whole time or the good people of this town might just be able to identify your charred remains when they dig through the ruins of this office."

Silence walked out of the door; the relief at being out of the cell tempered by his continuing to be held at gunpoint. Roberts pushed him in the small of the back to let him know to walk around the back of the sheriff's office. It being a small, detached block, they were quickly away from the main street and into the unlit space between the rest of the buildings that made up the small town. He heard Roberts behind him emptying more oil as they walked along.

Not intending to stay captive any longer than he had to, Silence looked around for anything he could use against Roberts. There was a horse trough and a few upright posts to mark the corners of properties. After about fifty yards, they came to a halt.

"Keep facing that way," Roberts said.

"Why would you free me now after going to all that trouble to get me put in jail?" Silence asked.

"I don't remember it being too much trouble at all." Roberts laughed in a sly way as he spoke. "It seemed to be both a pleasure and none too much effort, as I recall."

"Shooting men in the back?"

"They were no good. Amateurs. I'm surprised to hear you being bothered about their deaths, given what they tried to do to that pretty woman you're kinda friendly with."

"It bothers me if I get in trouble with the law for something I didn't do."

"I guess you were just in the wrong place at the wrong time. Funny how these things can keep happening."

This time, Silence anticipated what was about to come. Rather than turning round to check, he acted intuitively and stepped away from Roberts.

Turning now, he saw that the gunman had just missed, by inches, clubbing him with the handle of a revolver. Silence aimed his right fist at Roberts's midriff which connected and succeeded, judging by the groan, in winding the man who was now bent slightly forward.

Following up, Silence grabbed Roberts's head and brought his knee into his face. He heard a cracking sound, which experience told him was Roberts's nose breaking.

Roberts had dropped the revolver. Silence kicked the injured man's legs out from under him, and hearing another groan, picked up the gun from the floor and aimed it at his former captor.

"Now, you weren't about to kill a man with no gun to defend himself with, were you, Mr. Silence?" Van Hook's voice cut through the darkness.

"I wasn't," said Silence. "But I saw no reason to let myself be used again." He looked up and saw that Van Hook was standing about twenty yards away. The new arrival was holding a rifle, but had not yet brought it to bear on Silence. He was smoking a newly lit cigarette. "Your colleague, here, was about to knock me out so I could be used as a dupe again; but then, I'm sure you already knew that. What is it I was going to be set up for this time?"

"Well, given your recent residence, the good people of Madison Springs shouldn't take too much persuading that you would want to burn down the sheriff's office. Of course, they may also be willing to believe you knew the sheriff was in there when the fire started. No love lost between you and Sheriff Bolton, I understand. Could lead people to think you killed him deliberately. Still, I'm sure they'll give you a fair trial."

"What has Decker got against me?"

Van Hook laughed quietly.

"Nothing, as far as I know. You're just in the wrong place at the wrong time. A stranger who has the appearance of a killer about him. The perfect scapegoat."

Van Hook took the cigarette from his mouth and held it away from his body.

"Of course, you could always try and stop the fire before it gets too bad." Van Hook dropped the cigarette into the pool of flammable liquid that Roberts had laid down. For a few moments, it looked like nothing was going to happen, but then tongues of flame leapt up and spread back along the trail that led to the sheriff's office.

Silence ran toward the building in which he had recently been held prisoner. He was not quick enough to overtake the rapidly moving line of flames, but he managed to reach the office before the fire started to do significant damage to the building. He went to the front and entered with the intention of helping Bolton to get out in time. The sheriff was in his chair behind the desk; his feet propped up on the desk in front of him and his eyes closed.

The room stank of the same odour of cheap whisky that had been used on Silence when the sheriff had found him days earlier. When he got close enough to try and wake Bolton, Silence saw that he was more than unconscious. Below the chair was a large pool of blood which was still being added to by regular drips of dark red liquid from two holes in his back; large enough and deep enough to have penetrated to his vital organs. The man was dead.

The door to the back room was still open, and Silence went in quickly to grab the ratty single blanket that had been provided for him. He went back out and used this to try to smother the fire, which was now beginning its work on the building, quietly eating away at the sun-dried wood but not yet giving off enough flames to have raised an alarm in the small hours of the morning. The bottom of the planks had already caught fire, but it was small enough that Silence was able to beat it down with the aid of the blanket. He'd saved the building, for what it was worth, but not the man who had filled the office.

Silence walked back to where he had fought with Roberts, but no one was there. No surprise, really. Van Hook had, no doubt, dragged him off, though possibly not so far that he was not still being watched from some corner of darkness.

The possibility of handing himself in to Bolton's deputy was dismissed by Silence quickly. That would only result in him being returned to the cell, and this time, with the added charge of killing the sheriff. He rated his chances of being acquitted by a jury of men who had voted Bolton into office as low.

Apart from that, he was getting heartily sick of being used by Decker and Van Hook and needed to use his liberty to start turning the tables. He'd come to Madison Springs looking for one man—Brady—who he believed to have wronged him. That list was now longer, and he intended to finish his business here.

Silence considered stealing Sheriff Bolton's horse from the open paddock in which he knew it was kept, its owner no longer having any use for it, but decided that he had enough of a task proving his innocence without adding actual crimes to his list.

His own horse was locked up in the blacksmith's yard and to wake him up now would look suspicious. It was going to be a long walk under a star-filled night sky, made longer by his desire to avoid the scattered buildings of the town as much as possible.

Chapter Ten

The sun had been up for less than an hour when Silence got close enough to Joan's farm to see that the sheriff's office wasn't the only place to have been set aflame in the night. The main barn had been reduced to a charred husk of its former self. The roof had collapsed into the centre and wisps of smoke rose up from several places.

He saw Joan sitting in a chair on the porch of the main house, a rifle across her knees. As he walked closer, she held the rifle up, but set it back down quickly when she recognised her visitor.

"I'd say you missed all the excitement last night, J.T., but I'm wondering if you didn't have some yourself, given you were still locked up last thing I knew."

Silence crossed the open space toward Joan. As he got closer, he could see the streaks of grime and sweat that covered her face. Her hair was tied back, but had not been combed. She'd clearly been standing watch all night in case whoever had set fire to the barn returned.

Silence looked around. Apart from the barn, the rest of the buildings looked undamaged. He saw that the horses and the milking cows were out in the one field that had any kind of a fence around it.

"I should have been here, Joan. I'm sorry."

"The boy's dog gave us the alarm. Could have been a lot worse. I had a look around as soon as the sun came up. Looks like one rider. Probably would have set fire to each of the buildings in turn if we hadn't been woken up."

"Are Cassie and Manny alright?"

"They're alive and slightly less angry than me, on account of they're generally nicer than I am. I sent them back to get some sleep once the fire was burned out. No point all of us being up." Joan looked at Silence for a few moments before speaking again. "Do I look as bad as you?"

Silence smiled briefly. "Two days in the same clothes, a fight, a fire and a long walk back from town," he said by way of explanation.

"If you want water to wash in you'll need to go to the stream for fresh," Joan said. "Not that the little water we had around made much difference in fighting the fire."

Silence looked around for the empty buckets. He picked up two and headed off to the stream. Once there, he filled the two buckets before stripping off his sweat-streaked clothes and plunged into the cold, refreshing water. He dressed again in the same clothes and headed back to the farm with the intention of getting some coffee brewing.

****

"So Bolton is dead now, too?" Cassie said. "Decker seems intent on covering his tracks."

"Damn clever," said Joan as she started collecting the breakfast plates from the table. "Stops Bolton from being able to inform about the killings, if he ever remembered he was supposed to be a lawman, and implicates J.T. at the same time."

"Maybe *too* clever," Cassie said. "He's pulled that trick twice now. It's going to put people off working for him."

"Not if everybody thinks I killed all those people." Silence sat back in his chair, not looking at any of the others. "The judge should arrive in town tomorrow. Manny needs to see him to establish his claim on his family's land." He turned toward the youth. "I'll ride with you as far as the outskirts of Madison Springs. Given that I'm now a fugitive, I'll have to leave you there. If you go straight to Captain Hawton, he'll make sure you get a fair hearing from the judge."

"So, what are you going to do, then?" Joan asked.

"The arrival of the judge in town should draw plenty of people. With everybody's attention in town it might be a good time to take another look at the Decker ranch."

Manny looked at the expression on Silence's face. The man was trying to smile reassuringly for the benefit of the women, but Manny could see something darker behind the smile.

****

The dark of night was broken only by the distant stars above and the scattering of fireflies nearer the ground. The forests were noisy with the sounds of crickets and occasional rustlings of larger animals. These were the sights and sounds that had been J.T. Silence's only companions on many nights past…and, he expected, in the future. They were trusted companions, if limited, bearing him no malice and bringing no painful memories to the fore of his consciousness. He recognized, too, the sound of the gun being cocked behind him.

"You're not going to shoot me after I did all your dishes for you, are you Joan?" Silence didn't turn around from his position on the front step of the farm house. He kept his focus on the shrouded woods that surrounded the open area between the house and the burnt down barn.

"I've come to take over watch. If you are planning on doing what I think you are over the next couple of days, then you need to get some sleep while you can."

Joan was surprised that Silence stood up at this first time of asking. He vacated the chair and raised his hat to her.

"I'll take you up on that," Silence said. "Besides, we're both fooling ourselves if we think we'll spot anyone out there before Manny's dog catches wind of them."

He kissed Joan on the cheek and went into the house.

****

Manny looked up from the main street of Madison Springs to the trees in the distance and wondered if J.T. was watching, or if he had already ridden off to his unspoken business elsewhere. He wasn't sure when he would see him next, and wondered what might happen before then.

The livery boy again promised to take good care of Manny's pony. He looked at Manny as if he wanted to ask him something. Only as he was walking away did it occur to Manny that the last time he had left the pony there he had been in company with the man who the town had been expecting to be tried for murder today. Judging by the noise and smell wafting out from the back of the livery yard, there were a good few visiting steeds being kept there. Plenty of visitors in town for the trial, and disappointed to find out that the suspect had disappeared.

Manny decided to find Captain Hawton as quickly as possible. Walking against the flow of the crowd, he noticed Sally from the saloon passing him a little way off. He thought she had seen him, too, but if so, she chose to ignore him. Captain Hawton sat in his heavy wheelchair on the decking in front of the saloon. He held out his hand for Manny to shake.

"If you walked past that crowd you'll know by now that the sheriff was killed last night," Hawton held Manny's eye as he spoke. "Though, maybe you knew about that before reaching town."

Manny nodded. "Mr. Silence was at the ranch last night. He didn't kill the sheriff."

"I never thought he did. Sheriff Bolton might have been stupid enough to force J.T. to kill him in self defence, but it's not J.T.'s style to leave a body to burn like that. Besides, I heard the sheriff drinking here late last night. I think Sally left with him."

Manny was surprised to find himself disappointed to hear that about the saloon girl.

"Sorry, Manny," Hawton continued. "I don't think she did anything by her own choosing. Roberts seems to have her under his power. Poor girl is probably scared to do anything other than what he says."

Manny's years in New York meant he was no innocent in understanding the lives people could find themselves living. The block his family lived on had girls plying their trades on three corners out of four. One had been a niece of one of the elders at the synagogue. The first time Manny had seen a grown man cry was when the girl's uncle had heard someone mention her name in front of him. Like the others, she was 'protected' by a man who took much of her income. He didn't like to think of Sally earning her money in the same way, but he recognised the likely truth.

"J.T. said Roberts broke him out of jail. Maybe he and Van

Hook killed the sheriff."

Captain Hawton nodded in agreement.

"Most likely. The trick is proving it." Hawton tapped his hand on the wheel rim of the chair. "However, in the meantime we need to go and see the judge about your property claim."

****

Judge Henderson had set up shop in the small school room which won him popularity with those too young to vote. The children of the town were using their extra day of liberty to chase each other up and down the street while the adults waited to hear what was going to happen about the sheriff.

Bolton's deputy had given Henderson a list of the more trivial cases waiting for him. These consisted of several cases of householders seeking compensation for damage to property from stray farm animals and a couple of instances of petty theft where the judge needed to confirm the fines previously handed out by Sheriff Bolton. Henderson perused the sheet slowly while the deputy tried to explain the clamour of the townspeople for some kind of official statement about the killing of the sheriff and the escaped suspect.

"Sounds like you need an undertaker and a posse respectively," the judge pronounced while still looking at the charge sheet. "You bring the man in and I'll try him for you. Better be quick, though. I leave for West Pines the day after tomorrow. Now, lunch first, I think—I'm told there's apple pie—and then we'll listen to some of these cases."

****

Manny helped push Captain Hawton's chair through the crowd, now thinner once it became clear the judge wasn't going to try J.T. in his absence. The deputy informed them that the judge would be hearing the criminal cases first, followed by those cases which involved two parties in conflict. Only after that would he be available for other legal business.

The captain suggested that Manny need not stay while the petty disputes were heard, but Manny found the process, if not the actual cases, fascinating.

Several times, the judge seemed to apply law based on his own opinion rather than citing any existing law. Each time, Manny looked at Captain Hawton to see if he also thought it odd. The captain usually shrugged, but once or twice whispered, "That's the way it works out here."

It wasn't the way it had worked in New York. The Jewish community there had arranged for some of the brighter young men to be trained as lawyers so they could defend themselves, though Manny remembered his father saying it just encouraged more litigation amongst themselves.

Here, the townspeople nodded, or even clapped, in approval of each judgment as it came. Gradually, it dawned on Manny that the judge might be applying some kind of common law based on his knowledge of the people of the Territory. If so, would that mean he would confirm his claim on his family's land?

Chapter Eleven

J.T. Silence tied the horse he'd borrowed from Joan to a low branch of a tree on the edge of a small clearing in the woodland adjacent to the Decker spread. He knew he might be a while and wanted to make sure the horse had access to both grass and shade while he was gone. He left enough length of rope to allow the horse to reach a tiny brook that ran along the side of the clearing. He also took off the saddle, knowing that would make a quick escape harder, but meaning the animal would be more comfortable. "Look after the horse and it will look after you" was a concept that Silence had found had worked well for him over the years.

Silence worked his way through the trees to find a good vantage point from where he could observe the buildings of the Decker ranch. This was made easier by what Silence assumed was Decker's pride in his own wealth. The land around the buildings had been cleared of any trees or shrubs. The land closest to the ranch was mostly paddock fields to use for breaking or riding horses.

He had a good view of the track along which he had ridden in, alone, and out, escorted, a few days earlier. He could also see the gate at which a man was stationed and, if his eyesight served him right from this distance, was whittling a piece of wood to pass the time.

Apart from that, the compound looked very quiet. He could not see into the stables from where he was but guessed that many of the hands would be at work in the fields or in town to see what the judge was going to do.

Not everyone who worked for Decker was a farm hand,

though. Silence knew now that Van Hook and Roberts were hired by Decker for their specialized skills. He also trusted in Captain Hawton's information that Brady was working for Decker in some capacity. The man had been a ranch foreman when he worked for Silence, but he doubted that was how he plied a trade these days. How many others could there be?

While the ranch could be observed quite clearly from where he was, the very lack of obstructions also meant it would be difficult to get closer without being seen. Having tried the open approach once with little gain, he wanted to scout things out more discreetly. In particular, he wanted to know where he could find Brady, but he also wanted to know more about what Decker was up to that had required threats and violence toward good people. He would have to wait until dusk and hope that those who had gone into town stayed on for a few drinks.

He was just about to return to check on the horse when he spotted a lone rider leaving the ranch—and not by the main track. He was riding fast and in Silence's direction.

Silence kept stock still while he waited to get a closer view. As the rider came closer, he saw that the man was, in fact, riding toward an opening in the woodland a few hundred feet to his left.

He also observed that the figure was...*female.*

Decker's daughter was obviously a better than competent horsewoman. She barely slowed the pace of the horse as she guided the beast into the wooded area.

Aware that she might discover his own horse, Silence stepped back from his vantage point and trod carefully back to the clearing. He found the horse grazing placidly on some of the higher tufts of grass at the edge of the clearing. Picking a fistful of fresh, green grass he used it to keep the horse content while he led it under the cover of the trees.

Through the trees, Silence saw the girl skirt the edge of the clearing and ride off deeper into the woods. He was briefly concerned when he heard her call out, until he saw her rise above a cluster of vegetation. She was asking the horse to jump obstacles; testing the skill of both rider and steed. Both passed the tests admirably, and then she was beyond sight and sound.

Not wanting to leave his horse in case the girl should come

back the same way, Silence decided to make use of some of the bread and cold meat that Joan had made him bring. He shared some with the horse and then washed his own meal down with water from his canteen. His thoughts about leading the horse across the clearing to the brook were halted by the sound of hooves on ground.

Decker's daughter had returned by the same route, but this time, she stopped and entered the clearing. She dismounted, took off the hat she was wearing, and patted the horse vigorously while praising it audibly. She led it to the brook and allowed it to drink for several minutes.

Once this was done, she let it wander free and the animal sniffed the ground and started picking out bits of grass to graze on. After each mouthful it raised its head and kept stock still for a few moments before returning to the business of eating.

Meanwhile, the girl had walked a few steps upstream to sit next to the brook. She cupped some water into her hands and took a quick drink. Silence watched carefully, while stroking the neck of his horse to keep it quiet.

The girl looked nineteen or twenty, Silence estimated, and quite sure of herself. Even a man such as himself who spent much of his life away from civilization could tell that the girl's clothes cost more per item than any ten belonging to Joan or Cassie. It was while he was observing that detail that the girl started unbuttoning her blouse. Once she had done that, she untied the scarf she wore around her neck and dipped it in the water. After squeezing excess water out of the material she applied it to her chest. First, she dabbed gently between her breasts, then under and around them. Silence told himself he was only watching because to move away now would risk giving himself away. It was an unconvincing argument.

The girl stood up, her blouse still undone. She walked over to her horse and whispered something into its ear. Only after she had mounted again did she put her clothes back to how they had been. She rode slowly to the edge of the clearing, turned halfway around in the saddle and lifted her hat in the direction of where Silence had believed he had been well hidden. He heard her laugh as she rode off.

By the time Silence had got back to his vantage point, Decker's daughter was a tiny figure taking her horse into the stables. It was about twenty minutes before she came out again, suggesting either that the hands were all still absent or that she preferred to rub down and feed her own horse. Given the control she had demonstrated as a rider, Silence suspected the latter.

He hoped also that her little show by the brook was her way of rebelling against her father. If so, there was a chance their relationship was not good and that she was not telling Decker, right at that moment, about the stranger she thought might be hiding out near the property. In any case, Silence decided to move his horse to another location before nightfall.

*****

The approach to the main ranch house was carefully planned. Silence had waited until an hour after sundown to make sure he had seen which windows were showing lights in the dark of night. He circled the whole cluster of buildings and approached from upwind so as not to alert any of the horses in the stables. He estimated that there were a handful of ranch hands in the bunkhouse. He had seen four men go in and out at different points earlier in the evening. There may have been more inside, but probably not many, given the solitary light that was visible through the single window next to the double-door entrance.

Silence had taken jobs on ranches over the years to pay his way as he had spent time tracking down his family's murderers. Sometimes music featured as the centre of the evening. Sometimes the bottle. Sometimes it was cards, which seemed to be the case here.

Moving past the bunkhouse and its low hubbub of card playing, Silence sought out the darkest shadows in which to get closer to the main house. Apart from the single-story office annex, in which he had met Decker on his previous visit, the house was built high. Silence crept right up to the outside wall of the only side that didn't show a light. He knelt below a window and took time to listen for sounds from inside. Standing slowly he looked inside. He could see just well enough to be able to tell that this was a store room of some kind. Clearly, no one was inside the room at that moment, although he heard some conversation which seemed to come from the internal door. He could make out enough words to suggest he was listening to a couple of female house servants, possibly the cook and the maid.

Silence edged along the side of the house and turned the corner. He was now looking along the back of the house. He could see three ground floor windows; two quite large and, between them, one narrow. He took three steps to reach the first window, and heard within the same voices he had just been listening to. Probably the kitchen.

He didn't need to risk being seen by looking in. He could picture in his mind the servants sitting around a basic table hoping they were done for the evening, but staying put in case their employer called on them.

The next window showed no light. Silence stood straight but could see nothing of the inside at all. Possibly the room was a scullery, or maybe even a water closet, if Decker had built the house to order. He pushed gently but firmly to see if there was a possible opening for him, but the window was sealed shut.

The final window along the back of the house showed only a dim light which, Silence saw when he reached it, was due to internal screens being shut. He could hear two voices clearly from this room, and one of them was Decker. The other voice was one Silence knew from his past. *Silas Brady.*

Silence forced himself to keep calm even though he wanted to bust in and get the man he had been trying to find for so long. Acting prematurely now might ruin the best chance he was likely to get. He listened in to their conversation.

"My source close to the judge says he is likely to require the boy to establish a physical presence at the Nussbaum claim before he will give a ruling in his favour," Decker said.

"That place is a farmer's graveyard," Brady replied. "One boy on his own—he'll sell to the first person that makes him any kind of offer."

"Judge'll probably ask him to establish a presence for a month. Too long for my purposes. If Carlson and the others had done their job properly, ownership would have defaulted to the Territory and I could already have bought the land nice and legally."

"So what do you want me to do?" Brady asked.

"Finish the job. After your visit to the Adams ranch, those women aren't going to risk leaving their place unattended. Hawton can't get his wheels up in that valley. The boy will most likely ride up there on his own, even if the others try and talk him out of it. Should be easy enough to see he has a nasty accident."

"What about Silence? I can't believe he's really run off. He might go with the boy."

"Like I said, finish the job," Decker said with an air of finality. "I can ask Van Hook to do this if you don't think you can handle it."

"I'll do it."

Silence heard the door open and close, followed by the sound of a glass being turned upright and a bottle being opened. He left the lonely drinker to his task and made his way around the corner just in time to see Silas Brady step out of a side door and walk over to the bunkhouse.

The desire to confront Brady had receded. From what he had heard, it was clear that Brady was likely to seek him out. If he proved reticent, then Silence now knew where he could find him. Silence had also observed that Brady, his head presumably full of other matters, had left the door slightly ajar.

Silence decided to take advantage of the way now open. This was the doorway into the annex he had been in before. Despite the darkness inside, he could visualise from his memory where the other door was; the internal doorway that led into the rest of the house.

He paused at the second door and gave himself time for his eyes to grow accustomed to the dark—at least, as much as was possible. Just as he was about to try the door, a light shone through the small gap under the door. Someone, probably Decker, was walking in the next room away from this door.

Silence counted eleven strides before he heard another door open, and the light went out. He calculated that the next room must be a corridor from the number of strides he had heard. Pushing gently at the door, he found it swung open easily and the quiet swish of wood over a doorway rug was the only noise.

The corridor, if that is what it was, was almost completely dark with no light seeping in from anywhere. Silence felt along the wall until he came to what must be the door into the room where Decker and Brady had been in conference. It wasn't locked, and he let himself in and closed the door behind him weighing up the alternate risks of being enclosed in the room against letting an open door show someone was in here.

This room was just light enough to see due to the pale moonlight that the window screens were unable to completely block out. Silence slid the screens to one side, to gain better visibility, and undid the locks on the windows, affording himself another exit route. He then turned his attention to the contents of the room.

There was a desk and chair, smaller than the one in the outer office, as well as a bookcase and a bureau. Farther back in the room was an armchair and a small cupboard. The desk was clear on top. It had two drawers, one locked and one not. The bureau was also locked. The unlocked drawer contained only a pen, some spare ink and a key. The key did not fit the lock to the other drawer.

Silence was about to try it on the bureau when he heard quiet footsteps coming down the corridor outside. His mind raced. The footsteps were barefoot, not booted, and possibly a woman's. Clearly a resident of the house, as they had not needed to use a light in the dark hallway. There was neither time nor place to hide, so Silence put his hand on the knife he kept in his belt.

The door opened and Decker's daughter entered. She looked straight at Silence but said nothing. She was wearing a long white nightshift that covered everything but was thin enough to give a good impression of what lay beneath. With a smile, she walked over to the desk and took the keys out of J.T.'s hand.

"Looks like I'm not the only one wanting a little nightcap." With that, she turned around, went over to the small cupboard which she unlocked using the key, and took out a bottle of whisky and two glasses. She set both glasses on the desk and poured two small measures of whisky.

"I'd be more generous, but my father might notice the level

dropping," the girl said. "He rarely drinks himself, just keeps it for visitors he wants to put in a more relaxed frame of mind before he does business deals with them."

"Scotch," Silence said, gesturing to the label on the bottle. "Not easy to get out here."

The girl shrugged. "Scotch on the outside, Kentucky on the inside. Father refilled it. Still better than the stuff the hands pass out on."

Silence took a sip. The girl downed hers.

"Now, what are we both doing here?" Decker's daughter gave Silence a knowing look. "I'm here because my father doesn't like to see me drinking—a skill he would be disappointed to know was one of the many things I learned at the expensive Eastern school he packed me off to. Your presence might take a bit more explaining, but I'm certainly curious."

"I'm here because your father has hired a man who I believe allowed my wife and son to be murdered. I'm also here because your father keeps having people around here killed—and I'm curious to know why."

Decker's daughter sat down in the armchair. She crossed one leg over the other, her nightshift sliding up slightly to show most of one leg.

"My father is a bastard. If you think he has a more specific reason for his actions, you might find out more by looking in the bureau." The girl produced a key from the cupboard and threw it to Silence. He caught it cleanly and opened the bureau.

Apart from some fresh stationery, there was a bundle of papers tied up with string. Undoing the bundle, Silence found a map and several other documents. It only took a brief perusal to see what Decker was up to.

"Thank you Miss Decker."

Silence retied the bundle and placed them in exactly the position he had found them. He locked the bureau and tossed the key back.

"Rosanna," the girl said. "My mother chose my name for me."

"Is she—"

"Dead. Yes. When I was eight years old. I held her hand while she breathed her last. Dear Daddy was away—he told me he was working, but even then, I think I knew he was lying. My father mourned a whole morning before he went back to business."

Silence began to understand the young woman in front of him for the first time. He felt sympathy for her, but knew she would not thank him for showing it on his face.

"I hope you found information you can use to hurt him," Rosanna said.

Minutes later, Silence was making his way carefully back to his horse.

Chapter Twelve

"I'm sympathetic to your claim young man," Judge Henderson said as he looked at Manny across the school room table that was doubling up as a legal bench. The judge had finally cleared all the criminal cases the day before and only this morning was he hearing civil enquiries and disputes, much to the delight of the town children who had been told not to turn up until midday.

Manny sat on one of the chairs intended for the pupils while Captain Hawton had wheeled his chair down the central aisle of the room. Other people still waiting to see the judge sat only a few yards behind them, and neither Manny nor Hawton believed their conference with the judge would stay private for very long.

Henderson had looked at the document Manny held giving ownership of the land to the Nussbaum family. He had listened to the story of the loss of Manny's family which Manny had presented carefully without naming Decker specifically as the probable cause.

"The title claim you have specifies that the owners should take possession of the land in order to maintain ownership," the judge continued. "Even if you plan on selling, you need to live there for a period of time first—I'm going to say one month. Otherwise, ownership defaults back to the territory."

The judge leaned forward and beckoned for Manny to do the same. Hawton also moved forward as much as he was able.

Judge Henderson whispered. "You ought to know, son, that Frank Decker, who I believe you may feel is not your best friend in this town, is a close associate of one of the candidates for Governor when this territory gets to become a state. He may not want to wait a month to buy it from you nice and legal. I don't know if you've been out there yet but you may want to find out if it's worth trying too hard to hold onto."

Manny looked into the eyes of the judge. They showed signs of tiredness but there was also an alertness. Nor did the judge shy away from making eye contact.

"I can arrange for an officer of the territory court to come out and register your presence on the farm at the start and end of the thirty days. I'll even make sure that they send someone who knows how to handle a gun. Between times, unless the good captain, here, can help you out, you're on your own, son."

Manny, sensing that the judge had said his piece, glanced across at Captain Hawton who nodded, almost imperceptibly, to confirm that supposition. They gave their thanks and left the building.

****

The two figures sat together offered complete contrast to anyone passing by. Hawton, restricted to his wheelchair, had the stillness of a plains brave waiting to surprise prey. His eyes were keen and alert, while opposite him, Manny, a bundle of physical energy, looked downcast in the face.

"With no sheriff, and the judge leaving tomorrow, things have gone far enough for me to send for help. I'll wire a telegram this afternoon to Fort Calhoun for them to send someone. Technically, the army has no jurisdiction in towns, but the presence of some blue shirts may help to persuade Decker not to push his luck too much further. Of course, they are not likely to get here sooner than a week from now, which will make it potentially dangerous to spend time out at your family place if you insist on going out there."

Manny looked at the retired officer with gratitude. Hawton. Silence. Joan. Cassie. They had all done so much for him but even so, it looked like he was going to end up with nothing. No family, no land and no future.

"I know it may be pointless, but I feel I owe it to my parents to at least go and look at the land they wanted to make our home."

Hawton nodded. "We can probably hire a gig from the

blacksmith so I can ride out there with you. I've heard that valley is steep, and we may not be able to get all the way to your family's land, but maybe we can get close enough to take a fair look. I'm more than a little curious to see what all the fuss is about."

The rest of the day was taken up in visiting the telegraph office to send the message from Captain Hawton through to Fort Calhoun, and then negotiating a price for a gig which the captain could manage to drive alone should he need to.

Manny found the acts of doing something welcome, and kept his ongoing doubts about the usefulness of it all to himself. He had no faith in the rule of law in this wild, open country. Men like Decker bought or dictated their own law, while even the judge applied something that was barely more than common law. Nothing was certain.

With a plan in place to ride out to the Nussbaum property in the morning, Manny accepted Captain Hawton's offer of the couch in his hotel room—but he slept fitfully, at best. When he did finally achieve deep sleep, it was short-lived. A gently persistent tapping at the window woke him. Manny sat up and gathered his wits as he remembered where he was. He could see Captain Hawton was also waking up. The tapping continued. Manny got up and trod carefully across to the window. Standing to one side, he pulled back the frayed edge of the curtain to look out. While he could distinguish nothing more than the silhouetted outline of a man, Manny sensed straightaway who it was.

"Mr. Silence," Manny said in a low tone, "is that you?"

"It's me. Can you open up? I was hoping to speak to the captain."

Manny undid the latch and pushed the window out. Only afterward did it occur to him that J.T. managed to climb through the window without making any audible noise. By that time, Captain Hawton had lit a small candle which threw out just enough light for the three of them to see each other by. Manny secured the window shut again and turned to face J.T. Silence. Although he had the appearance of someone who had not eaten or washed in some while, he was otherwise alert, and even gave a hint of a smile.

"I was hoping to catch you here, Captain Hawton," Silence said. "Finding you here also, Manny, is a stroke of luck. What I have to say affects you most of all."

Without interrupting, Hawton poured Silence a glass of water from a small jug next to the bed. The water kept the dryness in J.T.'s throat at bay while he told Hawton and Manny about seeing Brady at Decker's.

On hearing that Silence had let Brady walk away, it was obvious to Manny that something important had kept his friend from acting.

"I think I know why Decker is so keen to buy your land, Manny," J.T. said quietly as he looked directly at the boy. "Seems someone at the railroad is planning a southern route across the Territory, so they can take the trains to the cattle rather than the other way around. They need to go through the hills somewhere along the long ridge, and their favoured route requires a new cutting through one of the lower points. Guess where that starts and finishes?"

Manny responded instantly. "From Miss Joan's farm through to my family's land?"

"You got it. The company will pay compensation at a decent price for the land. Probably more, with no disrespect to your family or Joan, than either place is worth as farmland. If Decker can buy both pieces of land, he not only gets to sell them off for a quick and tidy profit, but also gets to be a player in the development of the Territory. Once the Territory becomes a state, there will be new positions going for ambitious men. Senators and the like. From what I've seen of Decker, I've a feeling he craves that kind of prestige. He's been a big fish in a small pond and fancies he can do better still."

"And Brady?" asked Captain Hawton. "What are you going to do about him?"

"The way it looks to me is that everything comes back to Decker," Silence said. "He's at the root of it all. Getting to Brady, stopping attacks on Joan and Cassie, or trying to help Manny, here, well—the main barrier in each case is Decker."

Hawton nodded in response. "But thanks to you, we now have

a clearer idea of what he is trying to do."

"And thanks to Manny," Silence said quietly, "we have at least one possible place that we can frustrate him."

The hushed conversation continued just long enough to make arrangements for the following day, at which point, Silence indicated he better leave in enough time to get clear of town before the sun came up.

****

Silence kept to the north side of the buildings as he made his way back out of town. Although the streets were empty, the darkness of the dead of night had already given way to the quarter light that presaged the rising of the sun. He knew he had cut things a little fine for comfort as it was; people in these parts rose early for the start of the endless chores each day required.

Outside of town, including Joan and Cassie's farm, animals were already being fed and water being fetched. In town, the earliest risers were generally the most law abiding of the citizens, the ones least likely to be sleeping off a hangover. As a man currently wanted by the law, this was no real consolation for Silence. While the prospect of finding the likes of Brady or Van Hook trying to block his path was something he relished, he did not want to find himself in the position of facing down a brave, if misguided, dutiful citizen trying to bring him to justice.

As he skirted one of the buildings before he would be free of the town, Silence realised he was not the only one climbing in and out of buildings that night. Having dropped to lie on the ground as soon as he heard the sounds, he looked across the broad street to see Sally, the girl from the saloon, climbing into a basic, white-washed, one-story house via the window at the side.

Silence presumed it was the window to her room in her family home. Possibly her parents, if that was who she was trying to keep her movements secret from, were the only people in town who didn't know she was involved with Roberts.

It seemed more likely, at least to someone who had travelled through as many small towns as Silence had, that they knew but kept up the fiction of ignorance to avoid having to deal with the reality. Given Roberts's ability with a gun, that would be the safe option, for sure; but at the same time, they were losing their daughter a little bit more each day. Silence shrugged and thought to himself that it was not his concern...but at the back of his mind, he saw the face of his own, long dead, daughter.

Once he had gone past the last building, Silence left the road that headed toward Decker's ranch and carefully picked his way through some virgin woodland to the place where he had left his horse. He took some time to water and feed the horse before starting a small fire to make coffee for himself. The positive impression he had tried to give to Manny just a couple of hours earlier had disappeared. He was grim-faced as he looked into the orange heart of the fire.

The forces ranged against them were considerable, and his allies were two women, a boy, and an old man in a wheelchair who, while being a man of significant knowledge and connections, was not going to scare Decker when it came to a fight. And it would, Silence was now sure, come down to a fight.

There was a slim prospect of help arriving from the federal army following Captain Hawton's request, but Silence dismissed it as any kind of a possibility worth counting on. While Silence knew any message from Hawton would be taken seriously by the army, he also knew the ways of the army well enough to know that nothing happened instantaneously—which was the only way help could arrive in time.

Chapter Thirteen

Following an early breakfast at the saloon, served by the owner who was in a less than gregarious mood and complaining about the girl, Sally, being late in that morning, Manny pushed Captain Hawton's chair down the street to the blacksmith's yard. They had expected to be up before the town got busy, but there was already a sense of bustle and traffic around.

Manny suggested it might be the follow on from the judge's visit, but Hawton only frowned in response. The situation became clear when they got to the blacksmith.

"I don't know," the livery yard owner said. "Sheriff Bolton not even buried proper yet and the election for a new sheriff is called."

Manny shot a glance at the captain.

"Is that what all the fuss is about? I hadn't heard." Hawton paused but maintained a neutral expression. "Well, I'm just a visitor and have no vote here, but I'm interested to know who might be wanting that job."

The livery man, who had been tidying up some loose rope gave a strong pull to tie up one length.

"Man called Roberts. You may have seen him about; more than a hint of the hired gun about him." The livery owner hooked the rope over a nail high up in the wall. "Probably intended to have the effect of scaring anyone else off from running for the job. I expect it'll work, too. Shame, there are some good folks here as would make a decent sheriff instead of one working for just one ranch owner. Still, maybe something will happen to stop Roberts from becoming sheriff."

The livery man looked at Hawton but said no more. Hawton

moved the conversation on to the hire of a gig, or similar, that would take the two of them out to the Nussbaum's piece of land.

"There's a gig out back I can rig up for you, but it's real small," the livery man said. "Style mainly used by ladies going to church, but with a good horse it'll do the job. Only room for the two of you sitting though; no room for the chair, if you'll pardon my mentioning that."

Hawton assured the man that he didn't mind mention of the chair. Indeed, quite the opposite; it was when people went out of their way to avoid any mention of the wheelchair, which was often the case, that it seemed strange. A deal was struck for the hire of the gig and a suitable horse and the livery owner told them he'd have it ready in thirty minutes.

Hawton suggested to Manny that they use the time to walk along to the sheriff's office to see if they could find out anything more official about the election for a new sheriff.

The door of the sheriff's office did, indeed, have a printed sheet attached to the outside. There was a small gathering of townspeople crowded round, so Manny offered to work his way to get to see the notice.

"The man at the livery yard was right," Manny reported back. "There is a typewritten notice declaring an election for the vacant position of sheriff and inviting nominations. At the bottom of the sheet is a handwritten nomination for Roberts. He's been put forward by Decker."

"He must be very sure of his position to be willing to make his associations with the gunman so open."

By the time they arrived back at the blacksmith's, the gig was ready. It took both Manny and the blacksmith to lift Captain Hawton onto his seat and Manny wondered, as he climbed up from the other side into place next to the retired officer, if they were not making themselves more vulnerable. When they had met, just a few days ago, Manny had felt that Captain Hawton, for all his physical limitations, was a man in whom anyone could gain confidence from being in their company. Silence clearly trusted him completely. Now, however, Manny was beginning to wonder if, between them, they were facing more than the captain could manage.

That he was finally getting to see his family's land just reinforced the feeling that he was, despite the aid he had received from Silence, Hawton and others, alone in the world.

While Manny reflected, Captain Hawton took the reins of the gig and, with a short, high-pitched whistle, urged the horse forward. The response from the beast was instant and obedient. They rattled along the path out of town at a quicker pace than Manny had been expecting.

While this route out of town was new to him, leading to the other side of the hills than Joan's farm lay, it resembled the other road, the one that led to his family's makeshift graves. The trees, initially close together and giving a sense of being surrounded, gradually thinned out. An upward gradient in the track became more noticeable, and the vegetation increasingly broken up by rocks pushing up through the ground.

On several occasions, Captain Hawton had to stop the gig so that Manny could get out and move a stone from the path of the wheels. It was while watering the horse after during one such enforced stop that Silence appeared at their side.

"You'll be doing that every forty yards if you continue."

"J.T.," Hawton called out. "Have you ridden up farther?"

"Not the whole way. Just to where the track finally peters out to something not much clearer than a deer track."

"How much farther to my family's land?" asked Manny.

"Couple of miles, best guess, based on the maps I've seen of the area. Not that you'll get much farther in the gig, in any case."

Hawton sighed. "I'm more of a hindrance than a help out here. I'm sorry Manny. Looks like I'll not be able to take you to your land, after all."

"You can ride on with me, if you like," said Silence, looking at Manny. "Or you can head back to town with the captain, here. It's your choice, but if we do ride on, I'd suggest we travel slowly and vigilantly. I've seen signs of riders going up this track that look like they were made in the last day or so. We've not got too many friends around here, so I'd assume the worst."

"I want to go on, if you think we can travel safely," said Manny. "I need to see the land. I know it's not likely to be anything special but I feel I've got to see it, at least."

"Okay, Manny. Help me turn the gig around so the captain can travel back down, and then we'll go and have a look at this piece of earth that everyone seems to want."

Manny unhooked the horse and held it while Silence held up the front of the gig and turned it carefully to face down the hill. Captain Hawton sat atop the gig while it was moved. He was not a heavy man, and the gig was small, but even so, the strength required by Silence to complete this operation must have been considerable.

Once the horse was harnessed once more, Captain Hawton made his apologies again and bid the horse on down the track.

Chapter Fourteen

The noonday sun was high overhead as Silence, on foot, led his horse between the pine trees. Manny followed, looking from side to side at the grasping tree roots that sprawled across the earth seeking what moisture they could find. They walked parallel to the path, which Silence had abandoned, when walking on the loose shale began to generate too much noise for his liking.

Manny looked ahead to see Silence gesturing him to halt. The rope of the horse was thrown back to him and Silence went on alone. This had happened a few times already, and they all knew the procedure now without uttering any sound.

"We're there," hissed Silence when he returned. "There is a plot marker just ahead, but there are also recent footprints. Two, possibly three, different people. We'll tie the horse up behind the trees back there and go on alone."

Following the example ahead of him, Manny ducked down to a squat walk as they neared the plot marker. It was nothing more than a wooden stake, albeit one hammered deep into the otherwise hard, unyielding ground. Carved at the top was a three figure number, and below that was nailed an official looking piece of paper, long since faded by the sun.

As Silence gestured for him to halt, Manny felt he was bowing before the legacy of his family—the shrine or gateway to their promised land. Looking further, he could see that they were at the top of a meadow of sorts that ran down to a fast flowing, narrow river. There were rocks piercing the grass at regular intervals, and even the tall grass looked the type that could cut skin if you ran through it. Manny pictured his family trying to turn this into farmland; the hours that would be required to dig out the boulders, attempt to plough and plant. His thoughts were interrupted by Silence pushing his head down toward the ground.

A bullet hit a rock three feet to Manny's left at the same instant that he heard the now-familiar sound of gunfire. A second shot kicked up dirt from the ground as Silence pushed Manny down the slope. They both rolled into a shallow hollow where Silence brought his own rifle up to his shoulder and fired off two rounds without seeming to aim at anything in particular.

"Heard the rifle hammer being pulled back just in time," Silence whispered. "If he's alone I think I can take him; he's no kind of a shot. If he's got a friend anywhere nearby, we're in trouble."

The sound of another shot echoed against the rock-strewn side of the valley. Manny didn't see where it hit but guessed was somewhere on the outside of the hollow.

"Stay here and stay low." Silence spoke in his normal voice, the need for stealth having passed.

Manny, his face down in the ground, sensed, rather than saw, Silence roll out of the hollow on the side that would take him farther down the slope.

****

Captain Hawton looked again at the man aiming a pistol square at the middle of his face. He willed himself not to blink or flinch. The barrel of the pistol was no more than six feet away, and Hawton could see that the hand holding the weapon was gripping the handle tight enough to make the knuckles white. Hawton knew the man was Brady, and his assumption that Brady would also know him was quickly confirmed.

"Captain Hawton," Brady drawled, clearly trying to show contempt for the military title. "I believe we have a mutual acquaintance. In fact, I think you were kind enough to let my old friend, J.T. Silence, know of my whereabouts. Mighty kind, sir, mighty kind."

"What do you want?"

"Money and women, mostly, but if you mean right now, well, I guess I'd like to show you my appreciation for letting Mr. Silence know I was in this neighbourhood. I could do that right away by putting a bullet straight through your skull. That'd please me, sure enough. However, my employer would prefer it if you just had a little accident."

Brady shifted the aim of his pistol from Hawton down to the spokes of the gig.

"Now, if I shoot one of these little spokes clear away, my guess is the wheel will collapse before you go much farther. Same time, that horse, hearing a gunshot so close, is apt to run off as quick as can be. I should think you'll go shooting off the first corner you come to. Of course, I'll follow along, just to make sure."

A shot came, not from Brady's pistol, but from farther up the track where Hawton had last spoken to Silence and Manny. Brady was caught by surprise, and Hawton took advantage while he could, pulling a Derringer from his inside pocket and firing as soon as the short barrel was pointing at his would-be assassin.

At the short range, the small gun was powerful enough. Brady recoiled backward, clutching his face and falling from his horse. Hawton just had time to look to see blood seeping from between Brady's fingers before his own rented horse did just as Brady had predicted and darted forward in reaction to the noise.

In the blur of activity that followed, Hawton thought he heard more shots from higher up the track, but was more occupied trying to stay on the gig and keeping hold of the reins in the hope that the horse would slow up soon. The hope was in vain; if anything, the horse panicked even more as it galloped down the narrow, rocky track.

A fallen tree that would normally have aided travellers by marking the edge of the track where it veered around a corner instead became a hazard for the hurtling gig. The horse ran straight into it and jumped forward, achieving its ambition of freeing itself from the gig even as its legs failed to make controlled contact with the ground. The gig overturned and Hawton was ejected, rolling down the hillside until, at speed, he was stopped by forcefully hitting a tree stump.

Hawton opened his eyes, not sure at which point he had actually closed them, and tried to make sense of what had just happened. The gig, he saw, was so much firewood. The horse, about ten yards away, was making pathetic whinnying sounds. Hawton could see from the way one of the legs was bent in an unnatural way that the horse would have to be put down, if nature did not take care of its own before anyone could attend to the deed. He did not think Brady was likely to have survived the shot to the face but, for J.T's sake, felt he should be certain.

With an agonising effort, he grasped the dry ground in front of him and started dragging himself, only inches at a time, up the hill toward the track.

****

Silence sought the steepest gradient to give himself cover from the point from which the shots at them had been aimed. Once he felt sure he was out of sight, he moved as quickly as he could to circle about ninety degrees before starting to climb up again, looking for suitable vantage points as he went. He reached the upper part of the slope just as another shot was fired at the hollow. Silence could see the gunman about sixty yards away, taking aim once more from the illusion of safety behind one of the few trees that didn't look in need of some hard rain.

Silence brought his own rifle up to aim.

"Drop it."

The hired gun turned his head enough to see Silence. His surprise was clear, but instead of dropping the rifle, he swung it round to fire wildly toward Silence. Before he could fire again, his dead body slumped to the ground. By the time Silence reached the body, there was a pool of blood below that had poured from the exit wound in his back.

Silence listened out for any sounds of an accomplice of the dead gunman but there were none. Once he was sure, he went to find Manny.

"Do you know who he is?" Manny asked.

"Worked for Decker," Silence replied. "When I first went out to Decker's ranch, this one was acting as armed guard at the entrance. Given he wasn't much of a shot, I'd guess he was just a ranch hand who got lured by the promise of higher wages for what he saw as easy work. Seeing the likes of Van Hook and

Roberts swaggering around like they own the place could have that effect on working hands." Silence rubbed his eyes. "Another life that Decker is responsible for."

Manny followed Silence as he walked back to the horse to fetch a shovel to dig a hole in the ground. Manny put his hand on the top of the shovel.

"Let me. You need to rest."

Silence looked surprised by the boldness of the statement from the boy, but knew he was right.

"As you like," Silence said. "You dig the grave and I'll see to the horse."

****

Captain Hawton turned on his side to get his mouth away from the ground; gasping for air. He had dragged himself back to the main track and could now see Brady sprawled on the dirt some way higher up the track. From a distance, he looked still, and probably dead, but Hawton knew he would have to haul himself along the track right up to the body. He flopped back on his front, trying to ignore the scratches he knew would become open cuts. His shirt was in shreds and even the smallest pebble that rose from the track dug straight into his body.

Reaching forward to grab the ground ahead of his face, Hawton started on his way along the track. The effort was agonizing, and every time he tried to gulp for air he took in dust, as well.

When he finally reached Brady, Hawton saw that the man's chest was still rising and dropping slowly. The already drying blood on the ground was turning black. Hawton pulled himself along until he was level with Brady's head. His own breathing was so heavy from his own exertions he could not hear anything from Brady, so he pulled at the head to turn the face toward his own.

Hawton's stomach turned at the sight of the right hand side of what was no longer Brady's face. The bullet had obviously entered through the eye, even as Brady tried to turn away, and had passed right through the side of his head. Hawton heard Brady hiss something. He put his ear to Brady's mouth to try and hear what he was trying to say.

"Tell Silence I looked after his farm for him. Tried to look after his woman, too, but she wouldn't let me get near. She sat at the back of church with the negro family sooner than sit next to me. I wasn't the only one in the town that had a problem with that. When the boys started drifting back from the South as the war ended, some of them didn't like what they heard about the woman who didn't stay with her own kind. Someone told me when I ought to be out of the way…the night it was going to happen. I took the hint, and the pieces of silver. They used her some before they killed her. If she'd let me keep her warm, none of this would have happened."

Brady opened the one eye he had left. It was almost completely bloodshot. He gritted his teeth.

"Tell Silence," Brady paused to gasp for breath. "Tell Silence he can go to hell. I'll be waiting for him."

Brady closed his eye and fell back into a state of unconsciousness, but not yet dead. Hawton believed he would probably live if he could be taken somewhere. The blood loss had stopped, the bullet appeared to have missed his brain, and the coherence of his words suggested he was not in shock.

Hawton looked around. He could not see Brady's horse, but the pistol Brady had been holding when Hawton shot him was on the ground a couple of yards away. Rolling over until he could reach it, he checked the number of bullets. There were five.

Hawton lay on his back and aimed the pistol straight up in the air. He fired three shots. Whoever had survived the shooting he had heard earlier would hear the sound of his gunfire—and hopefully investigate. He could only hope it was J.T. Silence.

****

Silence was standing next to his horse when he heard the three shots. They came from lower down the track, where Hawton had been headed.

"Sorry friend," Silence whispered to his horse, not long freshly watered and rubbed down. "Looks like I need you some more today after all."

When he found Manny, he saw that the boy had given up on

trying to dig a hole in the hard ground for the body and was, instead, covering the corpse up with stones; plentiful enough up here.

"It probably shows more respect than he deserves," Manny said, "but I think it right to do this."

"It's to your credit that you do." Silence told Manny to keep quiet while he investigated down the track.

****

Hawton had his eyes closed when he heard the unmistakable sound of horse shoes on the ground, heading toward him. He opened his eyes, but the horse was riding directly out of the low sun of the late afternoon. He could make out enough of a silhouette to know that the horse had a rider and was, therefore, not likely to be Brady's horse wandering back.

He also realised that the rider was coming up the track which was not the direction from which he expected Silence to arrive. The nearer they came, the more detail became clear. There was a second horse directly behind the first; this one without a rider. And the rider of the front horse was Van Hook.

"Hell," Van Hook said, a subtle mocking tone in his voice. "You gentlemen seem to have had something of a falling out, here. Is he dead?" Van Hook gestured to the still form of Brady.

"He's alive. If he can be seen to properly he may stay that way."

"Well, I guess we'll have to make sure he gets seen to then," Van Hook said. "You too, my military friend. I have to say, I'm impressed that you got the drop on him. Did you draw first?"

"No."

"Remarkable, sir. Of course, it might be even more impressive if you hadn't left yourself alone out here without any means of getting back to civilisation. You should be careful. You never know who you might meet in these parts."

Hawton listened to the veiled threat implied in Van Hook's conversation. "I was sure someone would come by once they heard the sounds of shooting." It didn't sound convincing to Hawton, even as he said the words.

"I'm not so sure," Van Hook said. "I tend to think a lot of folks, when they hear gunfire, up and go the opposite direction, wanting to avoid any trouble. Fortunately for you, I'm not afraid of a little shooting—and I like to be able to help my fellow Americans when I see them in need."

Van Hook got off his horse and walked over to inspect the unconscious Brady. Hawton noticed that he didn't show a flicker of reaction at the mess that was Brady's face.

"I don't think too many ladies are going to be wanting to spend too much time in his company anymore."

Van Hook came next to Hawton and helped him hold his head up a little while offering him some water from a canteen. The water was warm enough to suggest Van Hook had been in the saddle all day, but it was welcome, all the same. Once Hawton had had enough to revive him, Van Hook let him back to the ground with a gentleness that surprised Hawton.

"I can get you both back to town, but the ride will be somewhat undignified."

Van Hook picked up Brady and slung him across the rear horse. He took a piece of rope from Brady's own saddle and used it to tie Brady into place. He then came and picked up Hawton with one quick lift. He carried him across to his own horse and cast him across the front of the saddle.

"You'll excuse me, I hope, but I think this is the best way." Van Hook tied Hawton's hands together, then pulled the extra length of rope back to tie up to the pommel of the saddle. He did the same with Hawton's feet. Van Hook then climbed onto the horse and, taking a position behind the saddle, urged the horse forward down the track.

Hawton wondered if their destination was town, Decker's ranch, or somewhere else completely.

****

Silence had spotted the blood on the track from some distance away. The other signs were easy enough to read once he stepped down from his horse. At least two bodies had been sprawled on the ground close to the blood and there were tracks from at least two different horses. He very quickly found the wrecked gig he had not long since seen Captain Hawton leading. The horse that

Hawton had hired was close by and not yet dead. Silence used another bullet to put the poor beast out of its misery. Once he was astride his horse again he felt torn in two directions. He didn't want to leave Manny alone for much longer up the trail, but he didn't want to abandon Hawton to whatever fate was presently his.

He looked up at the position of the sun to calculate how much daylight he had left and decided to follow the Hawton route for as long as he could and still leave himself enough time to get back to Manny before dark.

****

When he did return to the Nussbaum property as night fell Silence was grateful that the dark masked the worry on his face he thought must be clear to all. Manny acknowledged his presence but otherwise kept quiet, giving Silence time to give his own account of what had obviously not been a successful ride.

After taking his time, busying himself with seeing to the horse and making a small fire, Silence explained his concern for Captain Hawton.

"We'll both go back, straightaway if you think it best," Manny said. "There's nothing here for me, anyway."

"Could be you'd be giving up on a piece of land that's worth quite a bit."

"More than the life of a friend?"

Silence gazed into the glow of the fire for a few moments before speaking. "You know, Manny, you are a credit to your family. With all you've been through, you still are willing to give up the little you might have for the benefit of others. I thank you for it. We'd best sleep here tonight and make a decision in the morning."

Chapter Fifteen

Captain Hawton woke to the aches and pains of the day before and suffered a split second of disorientation as to his surroundings before he remembered that he had been, somewhat to his surprise, deposited safely back at the saloon room by Van Hook late the night before. His chair was not in the room and he presumed it was still at the back of the livery yard where he had left it. He felt a need to do something, to act in some way that might make up for his feeling of having been a liability the day before. He heard sounds from the street outside, indicating that the morning was already past the first flush of youth.

Hawton called for Sally, who arrived quickly enough to arouse suspicions in his mind that she had been charged with keeping a close watch on him. Hawton requested some breakfast and asked if someone could retrieve his wheelchair from the livery yard. The saloon keeper brought him some food ten minutes later and informed him that Sally had gone to get his chair. Hawton used the time to inspect himself for bruises or cuts that might develop into anything more serious, and once he was satisfied that they were all fairly superficial, he dressed himself.

"The chair had already been taken away from the yard when I got there, Captain," Sally said, apologetically when she returned from the errand. "The deputy took it to the sheriff's office. Matt—er—Mister Roberts—is acting sheriff now." The girl spoke with some pride about the man Hawton, and most of town, knew she was sleeping with. "He's started doing the job without pay until the election is finished."

"How public-minded of him," Hawton replied, but the sarcasm in his voice was lost on the girl.

"Apparently you were involved in some kind of gunfight, Captain, and they want to be sure you won't go anywhere. Is it true? Did you shoot someone?"

"Nobody that wasn't trying to kill me first."

****

In the back of the sheriff's office, Van Hook looked down at the dead body of the man that Captain Hawton had shot. No flicker of emotion showed on his face as he threw away the rough pillow that he had been holding in his hands. There was little chance of a small town doctor this far west doing anything other than ascribing the death to the gunshot wound.

"You done yet?" Roberts voice called through from the front room.

"I'm done," Van Hook replied. "Looks like good old Captain Hawton killed Brady, after all. I expect the local sheriff will be wanting to hold him for questioning."

Roberts laughed as he looked at the wheelchair in the corner of his office. "Don't worry. He's not going anywhere."

Van Hook wandered through to the front room and helped himself to some coffee. "I'll ride out and report to Decker. You keep an eye on Hawton and anyone who tries to talk to him. I'm going to pick up Sally on the way; I've an idea how she might be of use to us."

Van Hook waited just long enough to see the signs of unease on Roberts's face at his last statement. The plan requiring the girl, Sally, was genuine enough, but it also gave him satisfaction to know that even Roberts was too scared of him to try and stop him taking his girl without asking.

****

Manny was washing out the coffee pot when Silence hissed for him to stay low and quiet. The reason soon became clear. Someone was riding up the trail, but making no attempt to be quiet about it. Silence gestured for Manny to head back toward the horse while he waited for the rider to appear.

When he came, the new arrival was something of a surprise to both Manny and Silence. Unlike most people Manny had seen since he had crossed the Mississippi, this man was wearing a European-style suit. He rode his horse at the front of the saddle rather than at the back in the western manner, and he seemed to be reading a book as he moved along. He was fairly young—somewhere in his mid-twenties, Manny would have guessed—with a pale complexion and blond hair just visible below a narrow-brimmed hat. The overall effect was of a young man trying to look more senior than anyone would otherwise take him for. To complete the entrance he was whistling a tune; not one that Manny recognized, but which he later discovered to be an English sea shanty.

Silence stepped into the path, rifle loosely held low in his hand, and hailed the newcomer.

"Welcome friend. This land is private property. May I ask your business?"

"Why, good day, sir," said the rider. "I'm seeking a Mr. Emanuel Nussbaum, who I believe to be a man of property in these parts."

Hearing the conversation from where he was hiding, Manny edged forward to make sure he caught everything. He presumed this was another attempt by Decker to buy the land.

"This is the Nussbaum land," Silence said. "How may we help you?"

"We?" the rider replied. "Then I take it you are neither alone, nor Mr. Nussbaum. Perhaps he is behind you where the bushes seem to be moving rather more than would be normal on such a still, sunny day."

"Perhaps," replied Silence. "My question remains."

Manny stepped out. "I'm Emanuel Nussbaum."

"Then I believe I can help you. I'm an assistant to Judge Henderson who asked me to come out and verify your presence on this land as part of establishing your ownership. I've got some documents for you to sign so that I can witness them in the flesh, and I ought to check the markers of the property, if they are still in place."

Silence and Manny looked at each other as their visitor continued to surprise them.

"You're here quicker than expected," Silence said. "The judge only left town a couple of days ago. Hardly enough time to get back to the territory capitol."

The rider got down from his horse, dusted himself off somewhat deliberately and held out a hand to Manny.

"Julian Bright, at your service. I finished another job early and met the judge while he was still on the road so he was able to give me the task straight away. I can show you my credentials if you are in doubt as to my authenticity."

Bright reached into an inside pocket for some papers which he then unfolded, ready for inspection. Silence was about to wave them away when Manny stepped forward to take them from the official.

"So, now what happens?" Manny asked.

"I inform the territory courts, in the person of Judge Henderson, that you have officially taken possession of your land. You stay put and, as long as nobody enters a reasonable counter claim, the land becomes fully recognised as yours in thirty days. Not exactly orthodox, and don't look for a precedent in the legal books, but they tend to make law on the hoof out this way. So long as it's seen to be fair, nobody complains too much."

"I think we might expect at least one rival claim," Silence said.

"Ah, Mr. Decker. Judge Henderson did apprise me of the local politics. I may be able to reassure you on that point, at least. The Judge, I can reveal, is not overly fond of the group at the capitol with which Mr. Decker is involved. I can't see him being able to make a successful counter claim that would trump your family's. The only thing that you will have to be careful about is not giving him reason to suggest you are abandoning the land."

"In other words, stay put for thirty days," said Manny.

Silence looked down at his rifle. "And if Decker can't get the land legally, then all the more reason for him to try illegal means."

Manny looked back toward the grave of the man Silence had shot the day before. *Would this land his family had sought, in order to build themselves a new life, be soaked with more blood before this was all finished?*

Chapter Sixteen

Rosanna Decker pulled her brush through her hair in the full knowledge that the long, dark locks were not really in need of further attention. She was still dressed in her night clothes despite the sun being close to its highpoint in the sky. The hair brushing was for the benefit of any servants that might look in, and the lack of day clothes was to allow her to send them speedily away. Her window was open and her attention was really on the conversation she could just about hear from the room below.

Her father's voice was easy to discern, but the visitor was harder; the voice lower pitched and less expressive. She knew who it was, though. Van Hook had been here often enough, and passed his eye over her figure, without displaying a hint of shame about it, on more than one occasion. At the moment, though, it was her father's voice that commanded the gunman's attention.

"If you think it'll work, then go ahead, but don't waste any more time. If the boy doesn't take the bait, well, you know what to do."

The response from Van Hook seemed to be something along the lines of "be my pleasure" as far as Rosanna Decker could make out.

"About time someone visited the two women again." Her father's voice was clear once more. "Just to make sure they are alright, of course."

Rosanna tried to hear more, but the voices became muffled and more distant. Probably her father showing the hired gunslinger out of the house. She knew her father respected Van

Hook's ability with a gun, and probably feared him because of it, but he also disliked having the men who worked for him inside his house. The nature of his conversation with Van Hook meant he felt it was not advisable to hold talks in the open, but he'd clearly got rid of the man as quickly as he could. It hadn't always been that way.

When Rosanna had been very young, the Decker ranch had only one building, and the few workers that they could afford had eaten with the family. Her father used to get his hands dirty in the right way.

Taking her riding clothes from the closet and placing them on her bed ready to change into, Rosanna next started to take off her night clothes. Her former headmistress had described her as impulsive in one of her reports to her father. She preferred to think of herself as decisive. Now, she decided, was the time to act.

****

Silence reined his horse in as they approached the junction of tracks which meant they were getting close to town. Gradually bringing the horse to a halt, he slid off and led it off the track and into the thickening woodlands. Julian Bright had offered to stay one day and night at the land claim with Manny. It was an offer which Silence had been reluctant to accept, although he had quickly judged that Bright was trustworthy.

As a judge of character, Silence had only ever made one mistake. It was Bright demonstrating his ability with a gun that had been the deciding factor. The bookish exterior was deceptive indeed. Bright was a fine shot. Whether he was as deadly an aim in a gun-to-gun situation remained to be seen, but combined with his authority as a judge's man, it might be enough to keep people at bay for one night.

As he reached the final covering trees from which he could see the scattering of buildings that were the town, Silence noticed Van Hook riding along a minor trail with the girl, Sally. If that was what it looked like, then it most likely meant Van Hook would be occupied long enough to allow him to get in to see if Captain Hawton was still alive.

****

Silence Rides Alone

Hawton was finishing an early lunch when he heard the light tapping at the window.

"Silence?" hissed Hawton.

"Yup."

"The window's not locked but you'll need to use something to pry it open. I'm pretty much immobile in here, J.T."

Silence used his knife to ease the window open enough for him to finish the job with his hands. As before, he eased himself in without making any noise of any significance, and then closed the window behind him.

Hawton looked across from the chair in which he had been made comfortable by Sally before Van Hook had called for her earlier.

"Decker's either getting bold or scared," Hawton spoke, after a few moments during which Silence took in the scene.

"Where is your chair?" Silence asked.

"Sheriff's office. Roberts has already made himself at home, even with the election being days off, yet. Sally said the two old deputies had been sent off to make sure the outlying farms are safe. Apparently, that dangerous killer, J.T. Silence, is in the area."

"I'll keep an eye out for him," Silence said. He offered a smile, albeit a grim one, at the shared joke.

A knock at the door brought the conversation to a halt. The handle turned without waiting for a reply. Silence, with neither time nor inclination to hide, swung his rifle up with startling speed and had the doorway covered by the time the saloon keeper was in the frame. The man took one look at the barrel barely three feet away from his face and dropped a glass of water he had been bringing in to his guest. Silence leant forward to pull the man further into the room before kicking the door shut. With one hand, Silence held the saloon owner by the scruff of his clothes at the throat, and with the other, he kept the rifle aimed at the man's midriff.

"You often take away your guest's wheelchairs?" Silence said, looking directly into his new captive's face.

"It wasn't me," the man replied, genuine concern over his own mortality clear upon his face. "Roberts took it away when the Captain was asleep. I couldn't do anything to stop him. He'd have killed me if I tried."

Silence continued to look directly into the man's face. The unblinking stare was more than the saloon keeper could stand and he dropped his gaze to the ground.

"Do you like what Roberts has done to this town?" Silence continued. "Do you like having him and Van Hook lord it over you the way they do? Do you like the liberties they've taken with the girl, Sally? Do her parents know what's been going on?"

Silence jabbed the barrel of the rifle into the man's gut before continuing.

"Now, Captain Hawton, here, has some very good friends in the U.S. Army who are likely to take offense at anyone they think has been interfering with his liberty. Army stockade ain't so nice a place as you got here."

Silence moved the rifle to one side so he could take a step closer to the saloon keeper and whisper his next statement right to his face.

"Of course, if anything happens to the captain, you'll be praying the U.S. Army finds you before I do—or a stockade will be the least of your worries. There's something of a reckoning coming to this town, and you need to think really carefully about which side you want to be seen to be standing on."

Finally, slowly and deliberately, Silence blinked.

"Now, how about you go and see about getting Captain Hawton his wheelchair back for him?"

The man stood still for a few moments before realising that he had been given permission to leave.

"Nice performance, J.T.," said Hawton after the saloon keeper had gone. "Possibly overdone, though. He's as likely to run for the hills as go and fetch my chair."

"It's all bluff, in any case. With you, the boy, and Joan and Cassie all spread out, I can't even protect people, never mind deal with Decker."

"Did any of us ask you for protection?" Hawton replied. "I certainly have not. The women never have. From what I've seen, Manny doesn't seem the type to do so, either. Stop worrying about what you *can't* do, J.T., and think about what you *can* do."

Chapter Seventeen

Sally undid the top two buttons of her blouse. According to what she had been told by Van Hook, the boy's camp was just a few minutes' walk ahead. She looked down at the bruise on her left wrist. Part of the story, Van Hook had told her. Damned if it didn't look like he'd enjoyed putting it there, though.

Not much further along the track, she halted her steps as she heard a voice she didn't recognise. Not the boy, nor the man Silence, either. More mature than the first and more refined than the latter.

"I said, give your name," the voice sounded out again.

"Sally," she called out, trying to sound audible and scared at the same time. Sounding scared didn't take any acting. She already felt out of her depth and she couldn't see that things were likely to go back to normal any time soon. "I'm here to give a message to Manny Nussbaum."

"Who's the message from?"

"Mr. Van Hook."

"Shout it out, then."

"Mr. Van Hook told me I should only give the message to him, not anyone else."

"Keep walking up the path. Be aware that there is a gun aimed at you every step of the way."

Sally walked forward warily. After a dozen or so paces, she became aware of the man sitting on a low, rocky outcrop to the right of the path. He stood out for several reasons. He looked better dressed than just about any other man Sally remembered meeting, including Frank Decker. He also looked cleaner, more handsome and well-mannered—the last point demonstrated by the way he was raising his hat to her with his left hand even as he was aiming a pistol at her with his right. Suddenly self-conscious about the amount of cleavage she had on show, Sally held an arm across her chest.

"Pleased to meet you, miss," the man said. "Julian Bright at your service, provided, of course, that any service I might render you would not conflict in any way with my duties to Judge Henderson and the laws of this fine territory."

Bright smiled and climbed, with easy agility, from the rock. The pistol was still aimed, casually, at the girl. He gestured for her to walk ahead of him and then followed her, a pace or two behind.

"Visitor," Bright called out. Moments later, they arrived at a campfire which was being tended to by Manny. "And a lady, too," Bright continued. "Pity we didn't have time to get the best china out."

Sally, aware she was being mocked, felt the color rising in her face and chest.

"I've got a message for you."

"Why don't you sit down and deliver it in comfort." Bright indicated a large, dry log which lay on its side near the small fire. As Manny was already squatting by the fire, it made sense to be on the same level. Deliberately, she bent forward to step over the log, giving Manny a direct view of where her blouse hung loose at the top. He was looking at her but didn't give any sign of leering. Once over the log she straightened up and sat back on the log. Julian Bright remained standing off to one side but close enough to hear any exchange of conversation.

"Hello, Sally," Manny said quietly. "Do you have a message from Captain Hawton?"

"No, sorry." Sally looked unsure. "I mean...I have seen him and he is still at the saloon, but no. My message is from Mr. Van Hook."

"What is it?"

"He said to ask you to come back to town to discuss your land claim here. He has new evidence that you need to see."

"If that is the case," Bright said, "he should take it to Judge Henderson. I could take it to him, if you like."

Sally saw the first tactic was not working. Van Hook had told her it probably wouldn't, although he had expected Silence to be the one protecting Manny, not this smooth-talking newcomer. Time to move on to the next thing she had been told to do.

"Please," Sally looked desperately into Manny's eyes. "Mr. Van Hook...he likes hurting people...hurting women." She held out the arm with the bruise. "He did this."

Manny's eyes blinked as he looked at the bruise. *Was it working?* Sally wondered. "And this, too," she said as she pulled her blouse down over her left shoulder to reveal another dark bruise, and a fair amount of flesh, as well.

Manny spoke slowly in reply. "I thought Mr. Roberts might be protecting you."

From where he stood, Bright noticed the girl flinch at Manny's statement. She was genuinely upset, but even so, this was a clumsy attempt at manipulating the boy.

"He's scared of Mr. Van Hook. Everybody is. You have to come down or he'll just get worse and worse. If you stay up here, he'll go out to the two women on that farm and kill them. He said to tell you that. And when he's done, he'll come up here and kill anyone he finds here."

It took much self-control on Manny's part not to react to any of the girl's talk. Somehow, he managed to respond in a calm voice.

"I buried eight people a few days ago. My family. My entire family. Mr. Van Hook can't do anything to hurt me. Tell him thank you for the message, but I'm staying here—and he's not welcome on my land."

"No!" Sally cried out. "If I go back without you, he'll kill me, and he'll still come and get you. You must come. *You must.*"

"Why don't you come back with me," a new voice joined in the conversation. "I think I can promise to keep you safe."

Manny looked around to see an attractive young woman in an expensive-looking riding outfit step carefully over some tree roots as she moved closer to the group. She held a riding crop in her left hand but had no weapon visible. He didn't need to look across to know that Bright and the girl, Sally, were also gazing at the entrance being made.

"Hope I'm not disturbing anything, gentlemen," the young woman said as she smiled disarmingly at first Manny, then Julian Bright. Her next comment was directed at Sally. "I've got a pin you can borrow for that blouse, if you've lost a button there."

Sally declined the offer and set about doing up the upper buttons on her blouse.

"You'll be Mr. Manny Nussbaum."

Manny nodded.

"And I'm sure you'll introduce me to your friends, here."

Manny gave her the names of Bright and Sally. The young woman gave a nod of her head to each in turn.

"Now, I think you have the advantage on us, young lady," said Bright.

"A rare, but pleasant, position for a woman to be in out here in the Territories." A brief hesitation, then "My name is Rosanna Decker."

Manny made a conscious effort not to react too quickly.

"Yes, I thought that would get a reaction. I suppose Mr. Silence didn't mention that we met. No? How interesting. I suppose I can see why he might have found the circumstances awkward to put into words. So, now I suppose you are wondering what I'm doing here. But, of course, the question you two gentlemen should really be asking yourselves is how I got so close without you knowing I was coming."

"I'm sure it was due to the gentle tread of your steps, ma'am," said Bright.

"Well, full marks for the attempt at charm, but somewhat patronizing—and, if you look at the hooves of my horse who brought me up here, plain wrong.

Manny smiled at seeing Bright lose out to the young woman, but remained concerned at both points she had raised.

"Would you have walked in if Mr. Silence had been here?" Manny asked, directly.

"Now, that is the kind of question you *should* be asking. I can see why Silence is making such an effort on your behalf. And the answer, by the way, is yes, I would have." Rosanna Decker put her free hand on her hip. "So, do I get offered a seat?"

Bright regained his composure and, standing up, gestured for her to take his space on the log seat.

"Have you been sent with a message for us, as well?" Bright asked.

"Only on my own behalf. My father, as I'm sure you have assumed by now, is indeed Frank Decker. He is also a bastard. Oh, sorry about the language—I forgot there was another lady present." Rosanna arched her eyebrow as she spoke.

"He deserves everything he has coming—if anyone has the nerve to dish it out," she continued. "Your Mr. Silence might be such a man. I want to help him, and I believe I can do that best by helping you. I've ridden these hills since I first rode a horse, which was about the same time I first walked, and can get around as well as anyone in the Territory; as evidenced by my arriving at your camp undetected. Perhaps if you were not otherwise distracted, you would have spotted me sooner."

Manny noticed the way Rosanna Decker was aiming asides at Sally. Did she really think that he or Bright would have fallen for the routine Sally had been trying to pull?

"The girl can come back with me," Rosanna said. "I can keep her safe at the family ranch. It will be, after all, the last place Van Hook or any of the others in my father's employ, think to look. That is, provided she is smart enough to keep quiet and out of sight."

Rosanna now looked directly at Sally. "So, *are* you smart enough...or do we let you ride back into that nice Mr. Van Hook's arms?" She turned to look at Manny, then across at Bright. "Because that is one thing she is likely to be right about. Van Hook is likely to kill her if she comes back empty-handed, but that may not be the first or only thing he does to her."

"It's not a bad idea. As far as Van Hook is concerned, only you and Sally are up here," Bright said to Manny. "If she doesn't come back he'll assume the two of you are, shall we say, getting on well. It'll buy us some time. So long as Miss Decker, here, can deliver her part of the plan."

****

The elegantly tall horse lifted each leg carefully over the roots and vines that rose up from the ground. Rosanna Decker rode watchfully aware of the lack of a real path ahead of her and the dead weight of the girl, Sally, riding close behind her.

"Why are you really doing this?" asked Sally.

"I told you. My father is a—"

"Yes, I heard you say that. But aren't you scared? You must know you can't win. You're father may not kill us both, but he hires enough men who can—and will—happily. Even Roberts is scared of Van Hook. That man is a killer. He likes it, and from what Roberts says he's good at it, as well."

"I don't plan on being on the losing side in all this," Rosanna replied.

"You mean that was all phony back there?"

Rosanna sighed. "No. You don't seem to get it. My father is going to lose. J.T. Silence and that boy, Manny, have the guts to stand up to my father—and I'm going to do all I can to help them beat him."

Chapter Eighteen

Captain Hawton patted the wheel of his chair as he watched the shadowy silhouette of J.T. Silence make his way out of town, avoiding the few spots where light from inside buildings cast out into the street. Van Hook and some of the others were in town, but Hawton had no doubt but that Silence could elude any crude patrols that might be around. They would be expecting him to be up in the hills, not right under their noses—or, at least, they would until the saloon keeper started speaking loosely as the evening and alcohol consumption progressed. Silence had, Hawton estimated, a couple of hours start.

Hawton himself did not plan on sleeping. He did not think Decker would have Van Hook kill him, but there was always a chance that one of the lesser hired guns might take it on himself to execute a perceived enemy of their boss in the hopes of getting himself a cash reward. Hawton closed the shutter on the window and tucked his hand under the blanket he had placed over his legs. He felt the reassurance of the handle of the Colt revolver and manoeuvred his chair so that it faced the locked door to his room. If there was an attempt to force an entry, he would make damn sure he took care of the first few before any assassination succeeded.

****

The decision about where he should ride to, either back to protect Manny or out to make sure Cassie and Joan were safe, was quickly made for him as he observed unexpected activity near the sheriff's office. The light of a single gaslight shone out from the open doorway of the law enforcement office. Three men—Silence recognised Roberts, but not the other two—were loading barrels onto the back of a cart. The job was quickly completed as the barrels were small in size and number—about six, Silence guessed.

One of the men hooked the cart up to a waiting horse; his own, Silence presumed, given that he then proceeded to step up into the saddle. Roberts and the other man disappeared out of the light, but quickly reappeared, leading their own horses. This was all done without any audible conversation between them. Roberts and the third man mounted their saddles and all three rode off in the direction of the trail that led to Old Joan's place.

Assuming the worst about the likely contents of the barrels, Silence ran quickly in the other direction to find his horse so that he could track and pass the three men before they reached the two women.

It was about halfway to Joan's that Silence heard the tell-tale sound of cart wheels rolling over the rough ground not far ahead of him. He slowed his horse so that he kept pace with the three riders but did not yet overtake them. There was little chance that he would be heard over the sound of the cart, and it gave him an opportunity to let his horse trot at an easier pace. He hoped Bright would be able to look after Manny long enough to allow him to see this through.

****

Roberts hissed just loud enough to let his two fellow riders know they were to come to a halt. As the wheels of the cart came to rest, the three men tried to look ahead of them, into the pitch dark of the tree-shrouded night. There were the usual noises of the night; the creaking of aging branches and small animal noises.

"Better not risk taking the cart or horses any further," Roberts spoke softly. "Don't want to spook any of the animals until we are close enough to make it too late for the women. Take a barrel each. We'll go on foot from here."

Roberts lifted the first barrel himself and started walking along the track assuming that the others would be close behind. The sudden sound of gunfire and a thud from somewhere in the tree above and behind him was enough to send him diving to the ground. The other two men dropped the barrels they had been holding and sought cover.

"Circle round, but watch for the gun flash when I try and draw him out. Drop him dead first chance you get. If that is who I think it is, we don't need to give him any more chances at drilling holes in us."

Roberts waited for the gunmen to move through the darkness before calling out.

"Who is it? Come out. Let me see you. There must be some kind of misunderstanding. I'm the acting sheriff around here, so you might want to settle this with words—not guns."

A voice from the depths called back in reply. "No need to talk. Just get back to town."

As soon as Roberts heard the voice, he fired blindly in the direction from which his best guess suggested the new arrival was hiding. After letting off two shots, he ducked behind the wagon where the other two had already sought shelter.

"That sounds like Silence's voice," said Roberts. "We might be able to do two jobs here for the price of one. I might have hit him but I'm not taking that for granted. You two circle around behind him, one each side."

Roberts stood up to shoot again in order to give his men cover to break away from the wagon. Returning fire seemed to come from a spot twenty or so yards away from where he had guessed Silence to be. He was surprised that none of the shots seemed to be closer to hitting the top of the wagon he now ducked back behind again. "Not even close, Silence," Roberts called out hoping to distract his enemy away from the two men he had sent to encircle him.

"I'm not aiming for you, Roberts," came the voice, closer now.

Too late, Roberts realised what Silence was doing as two bullets slammed into one of the barrels of gunpowder. Immediately, he jumped away from the wagon and ran for the nearest clump of bushes. He kept going, staggering as he ran through holes in the ground and tree roots, until he saw a flash of bright light in the corners of both eyes. The sound of the explosion followed almost instantly. Roberts stopped to gather his breath. He turned to look back where the wagon had been and thought he saw a flicker of movement in the darkness. He was about to raise his rifle when he heard Silence again.

"I think your two friends have already headed back to town. I'm going to give you ten seconds to throw down your gun and start walking away."

Roberts threw the gun down on the path, some way in front of him. He walked forward to where he thought the main track was, which turned out to be closer than he expected, all the time looking ahead to try to fix where he thought he had seen Silence. Just as he walked past his rifle he kicked it behind a tree which he then ran behind himself. He pulled the rifle up quickly, and fired off a shot. The flash of returning gunfire confirmed he had been right. His dying thought, as he realised that blood was spilling from a hole in his chest, was to wonder if he had managed to kill Silence; to take him down with him.

****

Silence looked down on Roberts's dead body. The man had tried to kill him, but Silence felt an obligation to see him buried. That would have to wait for later. Other things needed doing first, and if the body was eaten by scavenging animals in the meantime, well, that was that. The two remaining barrels of powder needed to be found and dragged up from where Roberts's men had dropped them. The wagon had suffered in the explosion and was in no fit state to be driven with or without weights. He had no way of fixing the barrels to his horse's saddle. The only remaining option was not his favoured choice but, needs must.

Silence found the first barrel and lifted it up to carry over one shoulder. At least, it was not too far to Joan and Cassie's. The thought of some home cooked breakfast encouraged him a little.

****

Joan dropped the plate of bacon down in front of J.T. Silence, then set a mug of coffee next to the plate.

"So, you've brought us two barrels of gunpowder that belong to someone else and you want to borrow a shovel so you can go and bury the body of the acting sheriff who was on his way here to drive us off our land using that very gunpowder?" Joan said as she poured coffee for Cassie and herself. The sun was, even now, only just beginning to rise over the valley to the east of the farm.

Silence knew Joan's gruff manner was not meant. They were grateful that he had stopped another intended attack on them.

"We'll need to get rid of the barrels," Cassie stated. "I don't think it's smart to be caught in possession of something we didn't pay for, especially given the current state of events, and I'm not too happy about the possibilities of what could be done with it if the wrong person found it here."

"I'll go and hide them somewhere in the foothills behind your land," Silence said. "Probably best if no one finds me, either."

"Where to next, J.T.?" Joan asked. "Do you think they will have tried something against Manny, as well?"

"More likely than not. He has help with him, but I'd rather be certain for myself that he's alright. I'm going to try over the hills. Harder route than going back through town, but less likely to draw attention to myself, and may even be able to take people by surprise."

****

"It's not much to look forward to, is it?" Cassie spoke as she approached Silence while he secured Roberts's body over the back of his horse. "Buried in the back of beyond by a man who killed him and not even any family present to say a prayer over him."

Silence said nothing but continued to tie the ropes linking Roberts's arms to the saddle.

"Did he have any family, J.T.?"

"Must have had once, I guess. Maybe still does, but not around here, I think. He was involved with that young girl works at the saloon. Might have a wife somewhere, but they can't exactly have been close, if he did. Parents? Would they really want to know that he ended up like this?"

"If someone I loved died," said Cassie, "I would want to know, no matter where or in what circumstances."

Silence nodded to the rocky slopes of the hills behind the farm. "I'll bury him under some rocks up there. If someone wants, they can come and get the body for reburial elsewhere. After all this is finished, it shouldn't be too difficult for them."

While Silence made his horse ready, Cassie brought him a full canteen of water as well as food, bread and fruit mainly, for his journey. "Should be enough for Manny and the new man, as well."

Cassie stood to watch as Silence rode his horse up toward the hills. There was no path and before long, she knew, Silence would have to dismount and lead the horse, finding the best way as he went. Her mother came out and stood beside her, but Cassie was too lost in thought to notice her.

"If you want to go after him, I can saddle the mule," Joan spoke quietly. "Mule'd probably find a better way than a horse. I can mind here alone, though I doubt we'll be bothered for a while until they work out what happened here last night. J.T. thinks he can do everything himself, but he's wrong. The way to beat men like Decker is to stand together, gather all the decent folk, and say we won't out up with this crap."

"Mother!" exclaimed Cassie.

"Oh, don't tell me you ain't said worse." Joan laughed while she spoke, but then turned serious again. "I mean it. Decker will send men against Manny, if he hasn't done so already. The judge's man might be good, but he's not likely to come off tops against Van Hook; if he was *that* good we would have heard of him. J.T. might be in time—and you might be, too—if you start off soon. All of you together might do the job."

Cassie looked round at Joan's face and then turned back to gaze up at the way that J.T. had gone. She was not likely to catch up to him, but she might, indeed, manage to get there soon enough to be of help.

"I've an idea," Cassie said. "Can you help me with a few things?" Without waiting for a reply, Cassie ran over to the barn to make some preparations. Joan smiled to herself and followed.

Chapter Nineteen

Rosanna Decker was used to making requests of the hands at the ranch and seeing them carried out. So long as she did not overplay her hand, she believed she had enough authority to enable her to subtly undermine her father's position.

She had arrived back after dark and had managed to get the girl Sally into the house and her room without anyone seeing. Sally had gradually become quieter and quieter as they had ridden back on trails barely worthy of the description. Rosanna thought she must have been living on her nerves as she had found out that Roberts was either disinclined or unable to protect her from Van Hook's intentions of using her as bait to get Manny down from his land.

She had seen Sally to bed in her room, and then had gone downstairs to see if she could find out more about what was going on. There was a light on in the dining room and she had found her father sitting alone, finishing off his evening meal. There was a half empty bottle of wine and an empty glass in front of him.

"You're in late, Rosanna," he said. "You may think you are the best rider in the Territory, but you still need to be careful. I worry when you're out after dark."

"Don't worry, everyone around here knows whose daughter I am. I don't think I'm in much danger from anyone."

"Well, stay away from the hills tomorrow if you ride out. The men are going to be doing some blasting up there. Wouldn't want you to get caught in a rock fall."

"That's good to know father. I'll be careful."

A knock at the door saved both father and daughter from

further conversation on the matter. The Mexican maid came into the dining room, lowered her head and told Decker that Mr. Van Hook was here.

"I'll see him on the porch. Bring us out some coffee."

Orders, not requests, Rosanna noted. *He barely even sees them as people any more.*

Once her father had left the room, Rosanna asked the maid if she wanted any help with making coffee. The maid looked horrified and Rosanna decided not to push the question. Instead, she took a book down from one of the shelves and went through into the afternoon room. It was dark, but she didn't turn a light on. She stepped softly across to a high-backed chair, opened the window behind it just slightly, and sat down. If her father and Van Hook stayed on the porch, she should be able to hear most of what they were saying.

"I sent Roberts and a couple of the boys out to see to the women," Van Hook said. "I've left a lookout on the path up to the Jewish boy's place, in case the girl manages to talk him down. If not, I'll go up in the morning and finish him. That's...if you still want me to?"

"Yes. I'm not going to risk him establishing a legal right up there. I've promised people I would deliver that land. I need the boy out of the way." Decker looked up at Van Hook. "Just make sure the body can't be identified afterward."

"About the right time of year for a little forest fire, perhaps."

Rosanna had heard enough, and staying within obvious earshot—while she felt she could talk her way out of it—was probably more trouble than was worthwhile. She had gone into the kitchen to tell the domestic staff she did not want to be disturbed again that evening and then climbed the stairs to return to her room. She found Sally still fast asleep, sprawled over the bed. Best to leave her to it.

Rosanna had watched Van Hook ride off back to town; he rarely stayed in the bunkhouse these days. Maybe he slept in the sheriff's office. Wherever he went, it suited Rosanna that he was out of the way for the time being. Wanting to be awake early in the morning, she had made herself as comfortable as she could in the dressing table chair. She slept, albeit fitfully.

SILENCE RIDES ALONE

****

Rosanna was up and out before sunrise. She had woken Sally up to tell her to stay put and not make any noise until she came back.

There were now about five hired guns left, apart from Van Hook. There were also about twenty regular hands employed by her father. Most of them were competent with a gun, and would use it in her father's service if he gave them orders. She guessed that most of them were sufficiently awed by Van Hook that they would also follow his orders. If she could get as many of the regular hands out of the way as possible, she would cut the odds against Manny and Silence and also save the lives of some decent enough men who were just trying to make a living.

As expected, Rosanna found some of the best of the real ranch hands already conscientiously starting some of the early morning routine work. She approached one hand who was checking the chicken coop for eggs, and asked him if he could go out and check the well on the south side of the property. She spoke to three hands who were finishing an early breakfast and told them her father had asked them to check the herd in the outer fields and keep them away from the hills as Van Hook might be doing some blasting up there today. A little truth with the fiction always worked well.

Rosanna had managed to send eight hands away on rogue errands that would keep them away from the ranch buildings until the afternoon by the time she saw a light on in her father's room and decided to return to her own room. She might not have done enough, but it should help. Now, she wanted to see if she could help to balance the scales a little on the other side.

Rosanna collected a generous breakfast and coffee from the kitchen and took it upstairs on a tray. Sally was awake when she reached her bedroom and they shared the breakfast between them.

"You've had a good sleep," Rosanna said to Sally. "Now it's time to go for a ride. You'll have to run off to the north by yourself and I'll pick you up once I'm clear of the main buildings. My father will want to tell me again to stay away from exactly the place where I intend to go."

Rosanna led the way through the house with Sally a few feet behind. Seeing her father walk past the bottom of the stairs while she was halfway down, Rosanna called out to him, but more for Sally's benefit so as to warn her to stay out of sight at the head of the stairs until he had gone past.

"Are you still planning on riding out today, Rosanna?" Decker asked in response.

"Just off to the north pastures. Don't worry, I'll stay out of the way of whatever it is your men are up to."

Seemingly satisfied, Decker continued on his way to his office. Rosanna waited a few moments before signalling Sally to come down. She led her through to the dining room, usually unused in the morning as it attracted no natural sunlight. Opening a window, she indicated for Sally to climb through.

"This faces away from any of the main ranch buildings but even so, keep down as much as possible. I'll saddle up my horse and meet you just beyond that old hickory tree you can see there. I may be a while, but stay out of sight as long as possible. I don't think I need to tell you what'll happen to you if Van Hook finds you first."

Sally jumped down to the ground and hitched her skirts up high enough to run freely. She looked around to check that no-one else was around, and then ran barefoot and fast in a way she hadn't done since before she developed breasts. Rosanna cursed silently as she watched Sally run upright. The girl was quick but made no attempt to keep down and use the cover of the long grass. She could only hope that there was nobody watching this side of the house. Sighing, she closed the window and looked at the wall above the fireplace. She saw what she wanted.

****

Manny watched Julian Bright divide the meager breakfast between two wooden plates. If they were to stay here for any length of time, it was food rather than water that was going to be an issue. The main river running down the valley was close enough, and there were at least a couple of other tributary streams that ran across the land. Such supplies of food as they each had, however, were running short.

"I could probably hunt up some meat," said Julian, "but I'm not sure I want to start shooting off a rifle and drawing any extra attention to ourselves if I don't have to."

"Somehow, I think we don't need to worry about it, really." Manny managed a philosophical smile as he spoke. "If they don't come up today, in force, to drive us out—or worse—then it will be tomorrow. They need me off the land. They've tried just about everything else. We know Decker has no qualms about having people killed. The choice we—or at least, I—have to make is whether to run or stay. Either way, I see no point in holding back on the breakfast."

"You're a smart kid." Julian laughed and emptied the rest of the beans onto Manny's plate. "So, what are you going to do?"

"You're already past the time the judge gave you to stay with me. I won't ask you to do more, and I know you might if I try and stay here on my own. I'll wait until mid-morning just in case Mr. Silence comes back. Otherwise, I'll ride quietly down through the trees and start making my way back east. I don't want anyone dying in my name. If Decker's men come up after that, they'll find the place empty...and, I suppose, they win."

"Well, in the meantime, the best place to make a defense is going to be from behind the rocky outcrop that looks down the main route up here. Two guns can hold off an initial advance. After that, if there are many of them, they'll just flank us, so if you want to stick with your plan of getting out, then the last realistic chance will be just after the first sortie of Decker's men turns back to work out the obvious. After that, they'll be all around us and probably in no mood to take prisoners."

Julian kicked out the fire and poured the remains of the coffee over the embers. He checked both his rifle and pistol to make sure they were fully loaded and then passed the pistol to Manny.

"I hope you don't have to use this," Julian said, "but if you do, use both hands and rest it on a rock to get a steady aim."

Few more words were spoken while they saddled the horses, ready in case they should need them quickly. Julian chose his spot in the rocks quickly and gestured to where he wanted Manny to place himself. Both had a good view down the path without being visible until someone was almost past them.

Manny looked down at the pistol in his hands. He was to the right, and some yards behind Julian. Had the judge's man placed him there for the reason he'd given, that it afforded them the widest possible area to lay down gunfire between them, or was it because he was being given the opportunity to back out more easily if things got hot?

The wait for something to happen was not long. Manny heard the clicking sound of horseshoes on ground just before he saw Julian glance across with a silent expression which he took to mean "here they come". He waited breathlessly until he could see two riders making their way slowly up the path. Manny knew Julian would have seen them already from his more advanced position, and that it would be wise to follow his lead as to when to take any action.

"Stop right there, gentlemen," Julian Bright called out. "This here is private property and you'll need to give a name and drop any guns before you come any farther."

Manny watched as the two men heard the voice. One of them, a bearded, slightly heavy man, was clearly pulling back on the reins of his horse to slow down any further movement to an absolute minimum. The other, younger and clean shaven, looked the more visibly surprised and was too busy looking around, eyes darting all over the place, to make any effort to stop his progress. His left hand was covering the pistol in the open holster at his side. He looked, Manny thought, all too eager to do something rather than talk.

The older man, riding now behind him, saw the nervousness of his colleague and seemed to utter something, inaudible to Manny, but clearly enough to stop his younger companion from pulling a gun just yet.

"Why don't you show yourselves?" the bearded man called back in return. "We just want to ask the Nussbaum boy to come and listen to Mr. Decker's new offer to him."

"Let Mr. Decker come up himself, and we'll listen to anything he has to say." Julian looked across at Manny while he spoke. He raised his eyebrows as if to suggest he had anticipated the approach.

"People come to see Mr. Decker; not the other way around.

You've got ten minutes to ride down, or we come in to escort you—personal style."

The two of them, somewhat awkwardly, tried to get their horses to walk backward down the track. Manny wondered if that indicated they were actually scared of coming up here.

They soon gave up and turned their horses in as tight a circle as they could, cantering downhill as quickly as safe riding would allow.

Julian whispered across, loudly enough for Manny to hear. "I think they must have assumed that I'm Mr. Silence. They will know the voice they just heard is not yours but don't have any idea I'm up here. Unfortunately, that may not work to our advantage. It'll probably mean a quick show of force in numbers. I doubt if we have more than a few minutes."

Manny pulled back the hammer on the pistol Julian had given him and aimed it straight down the track. He could see the marks made in the ground by the two gunmen's horses, and he adjusted his aim marginally to cover the area to the right as he looked down. That would leave Julian to cover the area to the left, nearer to him, and also meant that in the likelihood of him missing a target, there would probably be other riders behind who might stop a bullet instead.

For a fraction of a second, he wondered how on earth he had found himself in this position...but then, they came.

Manny was surprised at how the sound went from silence to cacophony within seconds. Shod horse hooves impacting on the hard ground, loose stones being kicked up against larger rocks, men shouting and shooting; all noises mingled together in an assault on the ears.

Manny glanced across at Julian who was holding his nerve until he judged the range right. Suddenly, he raised himself the merest of inches and fired off an aimed shot at the lead rider. Manny tried to copy the same action. He pushed himself up, against the voices inside screaming at him to keep down and hope it would all just go away, until he could see down the barrel of the pistol at the riders beyond. The lead rider was just entering his firing line. Manny pulled the trigger before he had time to think about it any further. He saw the rider go down and another entered the focus of his vision.

Manny fired again, but this time, the horse went down and the rider managed to jump down before he was trapped beneath the weight of the probably dying animal. Manny shifted his weight just enough to keep the dismounted rider roughly in line along the pistol sight. He shot again and saw the man step back, dropping his own gun and clutching with his left hand to his right arm.

Manny's mind processed the information like quicksilver. Not dead, but not able to hold a gun, either. Move on to the next threat.

To his right, Manny was aware of Julian firing off a succession of shots; the sounds were more distinct in his consciousness than the rest of the noise. The next rider on Manny's side of the track was urging his horse on and firing off shots from a pistol in quick succession. These seemed to be impacting on the rock wall above Manny's head which meant his position had been given away by the shots he had made. Manny fired again, but this time, the rider kept coming. He was only about ten yards away when Manny, aiming for the heart, saw that he had shot him in the face. The rider, his legs caught in the stirrups of his horse, slumped backward to lie awkwardly along the length of the beast as it galloped past Manny and on up the hill.

Manny was aware he had one bullet left until he needed to reload. He tried to widen his focus to glimpse the bigger picture of what was going on when he saw, in the furthest recesses of his peripheral vision, a familiar figure standing up on the rocks to the far side of Julian Bright.

J.T. Silence was firing shot after shot at the remaining gunmen who, Manny now realised, were quickly retreating back down the hill. The whole thing had probably lasted less than a minute, but the time before the attack was now a lifetime away to Manny; the life he lived before he had killed someone.

There were seven bodies sprawled on the ground as well as the still twitching body of the horse that Manny had accidentally shot. Only when he saw Julian climb out of his vantage point did Manny do likewise. He ran across to J.T. to thank him for coming back.

"I'm not sure I've really done you any favours, Manny," Silence said. "Now, they know there are three of us up here they'll come up again more carefully—probably try to flank us and pick us off from a distance. You probably could have slipped away quietly before this, but now, I think, they will want blood. Yours, and mine."

"That's what Julian said, about them trying to surround us."

"He seems to be an able man."

Silence looked across to where Julian had been checking on the bodies. He could see the judge's man was now standing above the horse. A shot rang out and the horse had one final spasm before lying completely still.

Manny felt a tear in the corner of his eye.

"I did that. It's my fault."

"It's to your credit that you feel the loss over a created being, but the fault lies with the man who made the decision to ride that horse up into likely gunfire. God knows, we abuse His beasts enough at the best of times, but taking advantage of the trust of a horse is poor thanks for the service they give."

Julian Bright had collected up any firearms he found on the dead bodies and was walking back toward Manny and Silence.

"I'd suggest we pull back to higher ground before they come again," Silence said. "I doubt if we have long."

"I've got a spot I picked out earlier," Bright said as he gestured to another rocky outcrop further up the track. "It gives a clear view most of the way around but with only three of us we can't expect to cover everything forever. Our chance of a quiet escape is probably gone, but we could still try and force a way through before they have a complete net around us."

"I think they'll come after us and we will have left ourselves more exposed," Silence said. "What do you think, Manny?"

Astonished that the man he looked up to was asking his opinion, Manny was momentarily stunned to silence. He needed to think a little, anyway.

"I've found out today that I don't much like killing people, even if they are trying to kill me first. But I think Mr. Silence is right. Decker's men will have been told to make sure there are no witnesses to what they are doing here. I know life seems to be cheap out here, but I'd guess even these men here..." Manny nodded toward the corpses on the ground, "...have friends or brothers who will now be wanting revenge, as well as Mr. Decker's money. If I thought I could run, I would. I'd happily give the land here to anyone if it would save more lives, but I don't think it works like that. I'm probably going to die today, so it might as well be on the land my family travelled two continents and an ocean to reach."

Silence and Bright stood listening. When Manny was done Silence gave him a wry smile and patted him on the back as they all walked up the hill.

"Don't be so quick to say farewell to the world, lad. We're not done for yet."

Bright led them to the place he had in mind for their last stand. The side facing down the main track was a steep rock face about ten feet high, while the back was a mound of earth that had been brought down the hill by rainfall and piled up behind the rocks. Lying across the mound was a fallen tree and it was between this and the top of the cliff that Bright suggested they place themselves.

"We should be able to keep them at bay here for a while. The trees start to get pretty sparse from here on up, so they can't get too close without us seeing them." He looked farther up the hill and pointed to the high ridge above them. "My main concern would be if they are smart enough, and willing to take the time, to get some men right up there. A good shot with a good enough rifle would be able to pick us off without us being able to do much about it."

"They won't find it easy," Silence replied. "I came over those hills to reach here. There's no natural paths, and a lot of loose stones. Couple of times, I would've come down the quick way if my horse hadn't whinnied a reluctance to follow me. Still, perhaps you better keep a look out that way, Manny."

Manny nodded. Was J.T. just keeping him away from having to shoot at anybody else? A canteen of water was passed around and they all drank, knowing it might be a while before they could do so again. Julian passed the captured guns around so that they all could keep shooting longer without having to reload.

Then, there was quiet. Without saying anything to that effect, the two older men took up their respective positions at each end of the fallen tree. Both could cover the track up the hill and each could also keep watch for anyone trying to reach them by coming round the sides. Manny sat with his back to a rock and the horizontal trunk of the tree in front of him, and started his vigil of the looming ridge behind them.

Chapter Twenty

Van Hook looked at the gathering of men in front of him and spat on the ground. He had started out with twenty men and had already lost eight. At least he still had the five other hired guns, who he felt would be more reliable in the job to be done.

"Okay, so now we know that there are three of them up there, and one of those just a boy."

"The boy shot Tucker right in the face," called out one of the ranch hands.

Van Hook gave him a menacing glare and the man spoke no more.

"I don't see any reason to make this easy for them," continued Van Hook. He looked around to see who had what guns. Most had both a rifle and a pistol. One of the hired guns had a recent issue army rifle. Van Hook wondered how he had come by it but did not ask. It was, to him, a good sign that the man had both the aptitude and lack of morality he was looking for. "Stewart, here, will work his way around the back and get up on that ridge behind them. Should be able to pick them off easily from up there."

He divided the rest of the group into three parties. The four remaining hired guns he split up with two each in the slightly smaller groups he sent to find their way to the right and left flanks of their target. Van Hook indicated that the rest would come with him and make another frontal approach, but this time on foot and using such cover as there was to avoid making themselves an easy target.

"No more talk. If you see them, kill them." Van Hook smiled widely, his less-than-white teeth showing.

Silence Rides Alone

****

Rosanna pulled back both hammers on the duelling pistol she had taken from above the fireplace in her father's dining room. She handed the piece to Sally, who took it gingerly.

"You've got two shots only in this, so use them well. If it comes to trouble, I doubt you'll get much of a chance to reload. Shoot twice, and then run like hell is the best tactic I can suggest."

"Why can't I just run now?" asked Sally. "I didn't want to be here in the first place."

Sally looked around her. They were halfway up the side approach of the hill where Rosanna had brought her down the day before. They had stopped for a short time to let the horse drink from a small, but clear, brook.

"You're here because I don't trust you to keep your mouth shut about my helping the people who are fighting against my father, and because I thought you might want to get your own back against Van Hook."

Rosanna checked, for the third time that morning, her own pistol, a small Derringer that her father had insisted she keep with her for shooting snakes while she was out riding. She also had the other of the pair of duelling pistols tucked in her belt, but had not yet pulled back the hammers in that one.

"We'll ride another ten minutes and then secure the horses and make the rest of the way on foot. Keep quiet from here on; my father's men could be anywhere and the state he has got them all in they are likely to shoot at anything they see move."

Sally maintained her reluctant and sullen expression as she remounted the horse behind Rosanna. She wondered about the girl in front of her. How did she seem to be so in control of her own life? Sally had never felt like she was in control of events around her and had assumed that was the way it was for women, but this Rosanna acted without any instructions from others, even against her own father. How could she be so defiant of Decker when most of the town feared him, or at least, the men who worked for him? Rosanna was maybe a year or so older than her, but Sally couldn't believe that she would ever be as assertive as the girl who now urged on the horse they both rode.

The train of thought was abruptly interrupted by the sudden

sounds of gunfire from higher up the hillside. There was a minute or so of multiple gunshot noises, and then quiet. Rosanna slid down from the horse straightaway and directed Sally to do the same. She then tied the horse to a solid looking tree, started walking, and turned around to beckon for Sally to follow her quickly. When Sally tried to start a question to the effect of why they should be going toward the sound of gunfire, Rosanna gave her a sharp look that clearly told her she should be silent from here on.

****

High up on the far side of the ridge, a mule hesitated in taking its next step when the sound of gunfire echoed through the air. Cassie gave it an encouraging pat on the rump to urge it to continue its way forward. The mule carried a load, but Cassie walked along next to the animal when there was enough space to do so, or behind, when the way narrowed such that it would be dangerous to continue other than in single file.

Hearing the brief burst of gunfire, which had an odd, staccato sound from this distance, Cassie wondered if she would be in time. Part of her hoped she would arrive to find everything had worked out alright without her assistance, but another part of her—that part that she felt most deeply, but least publicly—knew that she could not take the chance.

****

Julian Bright looked along the trunk of the fallen tree and caught the eye of J.T. Silence. Had he seen the flicker of movement by the rocks lower down, where the previous attack had taken place? Silence nodded, almost imperceptibly, that, yes, he had seen. Both men kept the place in sight along the barrels of their rifles while still watching to make sure there was no other movement to their sides.

Silence saw a branch shake near the same spot. He aimed carefully and fired. He knew he had not hit anyone, but it would have the effect of keeping whoever was there behind cover for a while. It was a pity to give their position away, but they needed to keep the attackers at bay. If they got too close, the weight of numbers would likely give them victory. Silence hoped that they could keep Decker's men pinned down, away from them, until nightfall, when he thought there was a good chance that some of them would decide enough was enough, they could get another job somewhere else in the Territory without having to get shot at, and drift off. He knew Van Hook would stick with it to the bitter end, but he would have to deal with that when the time came.

There was a further movement of the ground bushes off to the side. Silence heard a shot fired and then saw dust kick up from the ground a long way short of himself. That was good. If the men attacking wasted their bullets and efforts from too far way to make any difference, then so much the better. He heard Bright firing off a single shot from the other end of the tree. A brief look across told him that Bright had fired at someone attempting to flank them from his side.

****

Van Hook saw one of the ranch hands in front of him look round to see if he was still there. The disappointment was clear on the man's face when he realised that he was. Van Hook indicated for him to move forward to the next boulder. More afraid of the killer at his back than the possible death that was in front of him, the man stood suddenly and ran forward. He had managed to cross about three-quarters of the distance when he was felled by a shot from higher up the hill.

Van Hook, who had been watching the small cliff face above, rather than the running man, spotted the place where the shot had come from and aimed carefully. He fired off two rounds and then rolled sideways to another place of cover. Sure enough, another shot came back to thud into the ground just in front of where he had been.

He saw some of the other hands nearby starting to fire upward. Most of it stood little chance of hitting anyone up there, but the peppering of gunfire along the top of the cliffs would make it increasingly difficult for Silence and the others to fire down at them. Van Hook spotted the next place for him to run forward to, waited his moment, and made his move.

From the new position, he could see that the men he had sent around to the left flank were clearly in place and laying down enough gunfire to cause the defenders difficulty. He could not see the other flank from where he was. It seemed probable that, by now, his men would be in place there, as well. All that they needed to do was to gradually tighten the noose.

In front of him, Van Hook saw another hand, who had been lying on the ground, kneel up in order to get a better shot. The shot was fired, but the man fell to the ground again straight away. Van Hook saw blood seep out from beneath the body.

No movement of pain indicated the man was already dead. Still, Van Hook thought, they could afford to lose a few more. He aimed and fired, again, at the top of the cliff. He didn't know who the third man was, but he hoped he would be able to deliver the killing shot to Silence or the boy—preferably both—himself.

****

Rosanna pushed Sally down to the ground, possibly with a little more force than was strictly required. When Sally looked up, wide-eyed and angry, Rosanna put a finger to her lips and pointed to a man straight ahead of them. Sally recognised the man as one of Decker's regular ranch hands. One of the ones who used to try and grab her while she worked at the saloon.

Rosanna mimed for Sally to stay put—which the expression on Sally's face suggested she was more than happy to do—while she would go forward. The ranch hand was kneeling behind an irregularly shaped boulder and firing off the occasional shot toward a point some way ahead which Rosanna could not yet make out.

Feeling her throat dry as she inched her way forward, Rosanna was all too aware that if the man ahead was surprised he would probably shoot her before he realised she was the boss's daughter.

Every few seconds there was another gun shot from somewhere along the hillside, and she used the noise to cover each step she took. She was crouched low to the ground but kept looking up at the man ahead. If she could talk to him, she would try a variation on the tactic she had used earlier in the day to send her father's men all over the place. In this case, probably a fake message from Van Hook to go back for fresh orders. While she was still thinking up the best cover story, the man pulled his head back as a bullet slammed into the top of the boulder. His movement brought him around enough to catch sight of Rosanna. As she had feared, he started aiming his rifle before he realised who she was. A flicker of recognition crossed his face just as he was about to fire, and this was followed by another, more puzzled expression, as he realised he had been shot by the daughter of the man he worked for.

Sally came running up to where Rosanna was kneeling; smoke drifted out of the barrel of her pistol, and an obviously dead man lay at her feet. Rosanna was prying the rifle from the dead man's hands.

"You've killed him!" Sally hissed.

"Looks that way," replied Rosanna.

"Doesn't it bother you?"

"Not as much as I thought it would, actually."

Sally sat back on the ground, her mouth open in astonishment at the coolness, or perhaps coldness, of the young woman in front of her.

"Here, you can have this, as well," Rosanna said, as she passed the second duelling pistol to the saloon girl. She placed her own pistol in her belt and used her freed up hands to check the rifle she had taken from the dead man.

Sally's hands shook as she held the second heavy pistol. Rosanna was already starting to move forward. Sally, not wanting to be left with a corpse, was about to follow her when she heard a sound to her left.

Another man, this time one that Sally knew to be a hired gun, was crawling through some undergrowth and stopped as he took in the sight ahead of him. With Rosanna already having crept around the boulder, all the man could see was the dead ranch hand and Sally with a pair of duelling pistols in her hands. Unable to grasp his own gun quickly because of the thorns on the bush he was under, he cursed out toward Sally.

Fear gripped her. "Make it all go away," she was screaming to herself inside her head, "Go away!" Barely thinking about what she was doing, she aimed the cocked pistol at the man and pulled both triggers simultaneously. The recoil force of the gun threw Sally onto her back. By the time she had scrambled back to her feet, Rosanna had returned.

"Come this way," Rosanna said as she pulled Sally away from the two bodies. "Don't look back. Trust me, you don't want to see what you did."

****

Manny had maintained his watch of the ridge overlooking their position without seeing anyone. Occasionally, Bright or Silence had thrown him a gun with a shouted request for him to reload the weapon, which he had done and returned in as much haste as he could manage. The weapon Bright had given him had not been fired any more. There was no room for him to fire around either of the two men, and his one effort at trying to raise the barrel over the top of the mound had resulted in a quick barrage of bullets smacking into the rocks just above his head. He could see J.T. was having to shift his position more and more, often to allow him to aim in multiple directions. He sensed a greater amount of urgency about him as well. Were the attackers closing in now, so soon?

Manny had adopted a system of checking along the ridge from one end to the other and then going back again so that nowhere escaped his attention for too long. Suddenly, he realised that someone—and it seemed to be a man carrying a long rifle—was trying to climb up the steep hillside that led to the ridge.

Manny looked across to both J.T. and Julian, but both were concentrating intensely on repulsing the ever increasing gunfire which was being directed toward the hillock. Manny decided that, even though he knew there was no chance of hitting the climber, nor even that he desired to do so, he could fire a shot which would warn the man that he had been spotted and possibly also alert Silence and Bright that their defensive position was soon to be undermined.

Manny raised the pistol high and aimed for a point just below the climber, which, given the distance would probably fall much lower still. He let off the shot and waited to see if anything would happen. He felt disappointment as he saw that not only did the climber not even pause or look in Manny's direction but that his action had gone unnoticed by both Bright and Silence.

As Manny watched to see how quickly the climber was making his ascent, he realised that the amount of gunfire was starting to dwindle. He looked across to J.T. to see that he was keeping an eye down the main track, but no longer firing in that direction—although he was firing off the odd shot out toward the flank. At the other end, Bright seemed to suddenly be under even less pressure.

****

Rosanna watched as the ranch hand she had known since childhood crawled back down the hill. She knew that the mock request from Van Hook was not really plausible, and the man had not even asked what she was doing up here, but he had seemed quite glad to get away from the shooting party for the time being. Perhaps the man had known it for a lie from the start, and was just grateful for the opportunity.

Shortly before they had met the hand, they had passed one of the hired guns lying injured on the ground having been shot from one of the defenders up ahead. The man had asked for help. Rosanna had given him some water and then taken his gun away from him. He was clearly in no state to move, so that effectively meant that another of Van Hook's party was out of action.

So far as Rosanna could see, that left only one man on this part of the hill that was still working for Van Hook. Unfortunately, she could not see where he was.

****

Van Hook smiled as he saw the signal from his right telling him that the man, Stewart, had managed to gain a position on the ridge. He signalled to the men on either side of him to stop firing, and to pass the same message on to the others. While it was unlikely that the men on the flanks would all be in eyesight of someone else, they would work out what was going on by the gradual lessening of gunfire.

Looking at the short cliff face ahead, Van Hook wondered if Silence and the others had yet seen that they were now surrounded and could soon be picked off at will by the man on the ridge above them. In any case, it was now time to finish this. The sounds of gunfire all around them were dying out. Van Hook called out.

"Nussbaum!"

As expected, no reply came.

"Nussbaum! This is your last chance. I have men all around you. You know you cannot get out unless I say so. Throw out your guns and step out from there and I'll let you walk down the hill alive. I'll give you five minutes to talk it over in there."

Van Hook hoped they would accept the offer. He would enjoy the look of shock and betrayal on their faces as he shot them. He motioned for the men nearby to start creeping forward again while their quarry was consulting and not paying such close attention.

He held up a hand to alert them that they should be ready to begin firing again, but paused as he saw a rifle thrown out from the rocks. This was followed by another rifle and a pistol. Van Hook waited to see if anything further happened. Finally, another rifle was thrown out, this time from the other end of the cliff. He hissed to one of his men to go and collect them while he lined up his own rifle to offer covering fire.

The man he sent out walked about half way to the strewn weaponry when he stopped in his tracks, turned around, and sprinted back toward Van Hook.

"It's a trick," the man yelled. "The guns are from our own."

Van Hook swore loudly and signalled his men to start firing again. Those close to him did so instantly and he soon saw that some gunfire was coming into the cliff from the right flank. Nothing, though, seemed to be happening on the left flank. Van Hook fired at the left side of the rocks to make sure there was no chance of anyone getting out that way. In doing so, he was well placed to also see when his men on that side started firing again. He smiled as he heard a gunshot from where he thought they seemed to have been firing before the brief lull in the fight. The smile was abruptly terminated when he realised that the shot he had just heard had been fired in his direction. His initial thought that it was just a wild shot, given it seemed to thud into a tree branch high above him, was short lived when another shot from the same direction whistled closer by.

"I'll be damned if I'm going to be shot at by men that should be under my orders." Van Hook realised no one was within earshot of him. He waved to one of the ranch hands to indicate that he was going to circle around to the left.

****

A bullet slammed into the rock just above Julian Bright's head. He looked around to see a small figure high up against the ridge with a clear view down on them. He realised that Manny had been both shooting up at the ridge and also trying to shout at Silence and himself to let them know what was happening. He looked across at Silence and saw the same realisation on his face.

Silence looked across, and Bright saw a look of resignation on his face. Bright swore to himself. They had lasted out well, and he felt that they were close to driving all but Van Hook and one or two others like him away. Now, if the man on the ledge was anything close to a reasonable shot, and the way he had planted his first shot so close above his head suggested he was good, then the game was up. They could stay and get shot, try and run for it and still likely get shot, or they could surrender, with the probable result that Van Hook would still kill them all.

He looked again at Silence to see he showed any indication of which option he favoured, but Silence was still staring intently up at the ridge. When he saw a grim smile creep across the face of his new, and probably short-lived companion, he looked back at the ridge. The gunman was still there and looked to be aiming another careful shot directly at him.

Bright was ready to offer up a prayer to the God that he believed in whenever he was in mortal danger. Raising his eyes upward, before they settled on the skies above, he spotted what Silence had obviously already seen. At the very top of the ridge, some hundred feet above the gunman, was another figure. This one, if Bright could believe his eyes, looked like it might even be a woman. He watched in fascination at the actions of the new arrival. They appeared to be pushing something up to the edge of the cliff directly above the gunman. It would have to be soon and very accurate to save him from the gunman's next bullet.

****

Cassie lit the taper and ran back from the edge of the cliff as fast as she could. She reached the mule and pulled it back with her. Once she had gone as far as she thought she needed, she turned around to look at the barrel she had perched at the edge of the ridge. She barely had a second before it exploded. What happened next, she could not make out, as all she could see was a mass of dusty earth rising up to fill the air in front of her. Was that a loud crashing sound she heard or were her ears ringing from the sound of the explosion? She hoped she had done enough. She could do no more. If Manny and J.T. were still alive, they would need to finish the rest of this themselves.

****

Van Hook had just about made his way around to the left flank when he heard the massive explosion.
"What the—" he started, but the rest was lost beneath the louder sound as the top of the ridge seemed to pull itself away from the hillside and fall down into the valley. His man was under there somewhere, the rock fall having covered the whole of the narrow ridge.
The two explosions of noise had brought others out of their cover too, Van Hook noticed. Not far from him, he saw two girls—and not just any girls. One was Decker's daughter, and the other was the wench from the saloon.
Van Hook couldn't believe either of them would dare to shoot at him, but if it turned out they had, then boss's daughter or not, someone was going to pay a high price.
"I thought your daddy told you to stay away from this side of the valley."
Rosanna turned to see Van Hook walking toward them. He held his gun loose at his side, but held in such a way that, she assumed, he could swing it up and fire as quickly as he could think. She smiled at him.
"I'm a big girl. Sometimes, I don't do what I'm told."
"Maybe somebody needs to take you in hand," Van Hook

leered as he spoke. "Have you been firing that gun you have there, missy? Looks like it might be a touch warm to me. I'd hate to think you had been shooting at the wrong side by mistake."

"I don't think I have," Rosanna replied. "I don't like to waste ammunition. Maybe you could explain what is going on up here. Did you just try to blow up the hillside?"

"I don't know anything about that. Maybe we should go and ask the gentlemen over behind the rocks yonder what they know about it. I figure, if you walk ahead of me, they probably won't shoot at us—and then we can have a nice, peaceful conversation. Just put down those guns, first."

Seeing that Van Hook looked like he was itching for an excuse to hurt her, Rosanna complied. Sally had already dropped her duelling pistols as soon as she had seen the gunman. Both girls started to step tentatively toward the open ground in front of the rocks where Silence and the others were still behind cover. When they were about half-way, Van Hook called out.

"Nussbaum, Silence. I'll kill these girls one at a time unless you throw down your weapons and come out from behind there."

Rosanna saw J.T. Silence stand up, but with his rifle still held in both arms ready to fire. His eyes were on Van Hook and nothing else.

"Are you sure you want to do that? Mr. Decker may not take too kindly to having his daughter murdered by someone on his payroll."

Van Hook spat on the ground. "That's for what Decker thinks. I've had enough money from him to keep me going. This is personal, now. I'm not leaving this hill until the rest of you are dead or running away."

"Look around, Van Hook," Silence replied. "I don't see or hear anyone else here to support you. I think the rest of them high-tailed out of here when that hillside crashed down. You're on your own."

"You really think I ever needed any of them?"

Silence said nothing. He kept his gaze fixed on the gunman, conscious of the bullet that could find Rosanna's flesh in the blink of an eye. That Manny and Bright had also, now, stood up to make their presence known to Van Hook changed little. The gunman was faster than any of them, and probably quick enough to down two of them before the third might manage to get a shot off in reply.

Julian Bright spoke next. "If you feel that way about Mr. Decker, why not testify against him? If you were acting on orders, I'm sure the judge will give you a full pardon in return for seeing him convicted."

Behind Van Hook, Sally had managed to stop her hand shaking enough to pick up one of the duelling pistols. She had managed to pull back the hammer quietly, but as the final sound of it being cocked reached Van Hook's hearing, he wheeled around and slapped the gun out of her hand and into her face. She screamed as the gun went off.

Rosanna took advantage straightaway to fall to the ground, allowing J.T. a clear shot. Even as Van Hook returned to face them again, both Silence and Bright had managed to line up a clear shot each.

Silence squeezed off a shot from his Henry rifle fractionally before Van Hook also fired, but the gunman was too late, and his own shot was off target as he reeled backward with the force of the rifle bullet slamming into his chest. Rosanna saw that Van Hook released his own gun as he fell to the ground. She jumped up and ran across the few steps to kick the gun out of his reach and then ran across to see to Sally. By the time Silence and Bright reached the gunman, he was just a corpse lying atop a growing pool of blood.

"I'll get these bodies on to the horses," Bright said. "I think the townsfolk ought to see who needs burying."

Manny had walked across to join the others. He looked down at the body of the man so many had feared. "More blood running into the land my father bought. This wasn't the dream he had."

"There's no harm in having a dream for a good place to bring up a family," Silence said. "Just a pity the dreams so rarely come true."

****

From the top of the hill, Cassie looked down at the scene below. She had been able to follow what had happened while being frustrated at not being able to do anything more to help. When Van Hook had fallen, she had been looking at Silence to see if he had been hurt. Seeing now that only allies of Manny and Silence were left standing, she realised that she was breathing calmly again. The presence of the two girls had been a surprise to her, especially Decker's daughter, but she had clearly been working against Van Hook and for Silence.

Cassie looked forward to hearing more about that story, and she could only wonder what Decker himself would make of it when he found out. She had heard the Decker girl was strong-willed, like her father, and assumed she was of like mind to him.

The rock fall she had caused with the explosion had destroyed any semblance of a path down to where the others were. Cassie turned around to start her journey back to the farm, and then, an appointment in town.

Chapter Twenty-One

Frank Decker pulled back on the reins to slow the horses to a gradual halt. It had been a long time since he had switched from riding on one of his horses to riding in a gig when he needed to make a call in town. He found it more comfortable and, he felt, it reflected his station within the region to be conveyed by two horses rather than one.

He had timed his arrival to coincide with the posting up on the sheriff's office door of the notice that Acting Sheriff Roberts had been killed in an explosion while trying to protect the town. He would make a speech demanding more should be done to preserve law and order in the area, and following the expected positive response to his speech, he would then propose one of his men, supported by the full resources of the Decker ranch, to impose that order.

Decker left the gig and horses at the livery yard and walked the short distance to the sheriff's office. A small crowd was already gathering in front of the door trying to read the bill poster that Decker had told one of his hands to nail to the front door.

More people were starting to come out of nearby buildings, eager to find out what all the fuss was about. Decker waited while a bigger crown gradually built up. They were mostly struggling small holders, and when he finally walked forward to make his pitch, he did so in simple words, assuming they would not cope with more.

When he arrived at his final appeal for support to help clean up the town, he stepped back and tried to look humble while waiting for the shouts of agreement and support. Although he had only managed to find a couple of hands who were not assisting Van Hook up in the hills, he had arranged for those two to merge into the crowd and boost the calls for support for Decker's plan.

Decker heard some faltering words of agreement from places in the crowd, but they were otherwise quiet. The silence was broken by a woman's voice. *Was it one of the women from that ranch he heard?*

"We all know the cause of all the trouble in this valley Mr. Decker," the woman's voice called out. "It's you, and those so-called men you pay to do your dirty work for you."

Decker looked out and saw the woman who was speaking, standing alongside an older woman. *Her mother?* They were standing close to the wheelchair of Captain Hawton who had managed to persuade someone to help him down here. They must be the women he had tried to intimidate into selling their farm. Decker could see that neither looked much intimidated, at this point. Now, the older woman was starting to talk.

"If I was a man, if the damn law in this country said I could, I'd stand for sheriff myself. Maybe I can't do that, but I damn well know we don't need another sheriff in the pocket of Mr. Decker, here. You all know that his men tried to shoot and burn us off our farm. He claims to support the law. I say, *he* is the criminal here."

Decker could see the initiative was running away from him and made an attempt to grab it back.

"I can see you've obviously had a bad experience, madam, but I can assure you that I am not responsible for what you are suggesting and..." There was disbelieving laughter from some in the crowd. "...and you should be careful about making statements which could be libellous."

The laughter from the crowd was actually spreading. Mocking. *Mocking him.* Decker looked around. Even the two ranch hands were covering their faces to hide, Decker assumed, their own laughter. *Where was Van Hook? He should be here by now.*

Decker heard the sound of horses from the end of the street. He looked hopefully, but what he saw was a long way from what he expected and hoped for. The Nussbaum boy was riding along the street with the man, Silence, alongside him and another oddly dressed man. Another horse behind the three riders had a body slung across the saddle. Decker's eyes narrowed as he slowly realised that he was looking at the body, probably the corpse, of Van Hook. *Could no one be relied upon to do the job they were paid to do?*

The man Decker didn't recognise got down from his horse and led the fourth horse by the reins right up to where Decker was standing.

"My name is Julian Bright, and I work for Judge Henderson. I am here as a witness to report that the man on this horse, Van Hook by name, tried to drive this lad, Manny Nussbaum, off his land...and failing to do that, tried to kill him. I can tell you that Van Hook is now dead, killed in self-defence by Mr. J.T. Silence, here, and that I and several other witnesses, including Mr. Decker's own daughter, can testify that it was a fair fight. We brought the body here to turn over to the proper authorities, and I understand you good people are now in the business of electing a new sheriff—but as I believe Van Hook worked for *you*, Mr. Decker, you might be interested in taking care of his body."

Decker looked down at Van Hook's lifeless face. Bright had sunk him in a single speech. There was no chance now of getting either piece of land he needed before the news of the railroad became public. The crowd was clearly against him, and he had only a couple of men left—and neither of them real gun hands.

"Alright, Mr. Bright." Decker spoke softly, but the crowd heard each word. "Van Hook worked for me, that is known well enough, but we both worked for someone else. Let's have a talk about this, shall we, and see if we can come to some sort of arrangement? If you can get me to Judge Henderson, I can give him names."

****

Silence heard the shot—from a small pistol, his experience informed him—and saw the patch of blood grow larger and larger on the white shirt in front of the fallen Decker's heart. From atop his horse at the back of the crowd he could not see where the shot had come from.

All the people in the crowd were looking about them to see if they could see who had fired a gun, but no consensus was emerging. Bright held Decker by the shoulders and looked across to Silence with a shake of the head to let him know that Decker was dead.

Silence saw Manny slide from his horse and run over to Cassie and Joan. Louis ran around his feet, jumped up and licked his face. Beyond the happily reunited group of friends, he saw a slight figure in a baggy-sleeved black jacket walking away from the newly dead body while everyone else seemed to be wanting to get closer.

Silence kicked his heels into the flanks of his horse which started to trot in the direction of the figure. The man turned left into a side street. Silence reined his horse to follow, but as they rounded the corner, the side street was empty.

There were only three buildings on each side before the town ran out. The man was nowhere to be seen. Silence rode up and down the street several times with no further sight of the figure.

****

Rosanna Decker wore the customary black at the funeral for her father, the dark blouse accentuating her figure very effectively. J.T. Silence stood across from her with the custom-made coffin lying in the hole between them. To his right, Manny lowered his head in genuine respect for the man who had tried to have him killed. Captain Hawton was also there. Behind Rosanna were the remainder of Decker's ranch hands, all relieved at no longer being required to do anything but fixing fences and taking care of cattle.

Julian Bright had made his apologies in order to convey the news of what had happened to Judge Henderson as quickly as possible. Cassie had declined to attend, and Joan had said something more colourful in response to the suggestion that she might want to see Decker off.

The service was brief, and Decker's men took advantage of the visit to town to spend some money in the saloon. Rosanna seemed to be walking alongside Silence without anyone being aware that she was headed in his direction.

"Are you sure you won't reconsider my offer?"

"Which one?" Silence asked, one eyebrow raised.

Rosanna laughed briefly. "The one about coming to run my ranch for me."

"Your father offered me a job once."

"I know."

"I turned him down."

"I thought we were on the same side."

"Maybe we just had a common enemy." Silence smiled as he spoke. "I appreciate the help you gave us, but if I were to go back to running a ranch, it would have to be my own."

"I'm sure we could come to some sort of...partnership agreement." Rosanna's pupils widened as she looked Silence directly in the eye.

"I'm not ready to settle down again, and I'm certainly not ready for you. I wish you well, Miss Decker. I'm sure you'll be a success at whatever you set out to do."

"And I wish you well, Mr. Silence, for your future. Don't go and get yourself killed." Rosanna reached up and kissed Silence lightly on the lips. "Now, then, I must speak to that nice young Nussbaum boy before everyone goes."

****

Silence stood on the porch of Joan's farmhouse and watched Manny throw a stick for Louis to fetch. Manny looked as happy as Silence had seen him.

"We'll make it a good home for him," Cassie said as she came to stand alongside Silence. "It'll be good to have a boy about the place. He wanted to use the money the railroad company is offering him for the sale of his land to invest in this farm, but Mama told him to put it in the bank until he meets a decent girl, and that she'd settle for him chopping some firewood for us."

"Thank you for all you've done," Silence replied. "For him, and for me. We both owe you our lives, for one thing."

"You'd have thought of some way out, J.T."

"I'm not so sure. Van Hook had us where he wanted us. If it hadn't been for that explosion, we wouldn't all be here."

Cassie put her hand on top of J.T.'s and said, "Stay. Manny would love to have you around. I...I'd love to have you around."

"Not yet, Cassie. I'm sorry. If I was going to settle again, it would be here in this place. With you. But not yet. I still see her face every time I close my eyes. I'll ride a bit more, yet."

"What will you do, now that Brady is dead?"

"The captain has offered me some work."

Cassie wondered if Captain Hawton had offered first, or if Silence had asked, but she said no more. Silence leant down and kissed her on the forehead. Cassie closed her eyes. When she opened them again, J.T was climbing into the saddle of his horse and waving good-bye to Manny and her mother. Cassie stood and watched him ride slowly out of sight.

"Of course you see her face every time you close your eyes," she murmured. "I know exactly how that feels."

Acknowledgements

Many thanks to all the following who have supported the journey of this book.

First and foremost, to Elizabeth and Bethan for their encouragement.

To all the North Bristol Writers.

To the real Jay T. Silence for letting me borrow his name.

To Cheryl Pierson, Livia J. Washburn and Kathleen Rice Adams for making it happen.

About the Author

Charles Millsted was born in the East and travelled to live in the West; of England, that is. Having worked as a civil servant, summer camp counsellor (in Illinois), luggage salesman, finance industry administrator, teacher and film extra he is now writing in a range of genres. Recent short stories can be found in the anthologies 'Airship shape and Bristol Fashion', 'North by Southwest' and 'Challenger Unbound'. He also writes about comic books for 'Back Issue' magazine including contributing to their special western themed issue. Charles lives in Bristol, England with his wife and daughter. 'Silence Rides Alone' is his first western novel. There will be more.

More Westerns from Sundown Press

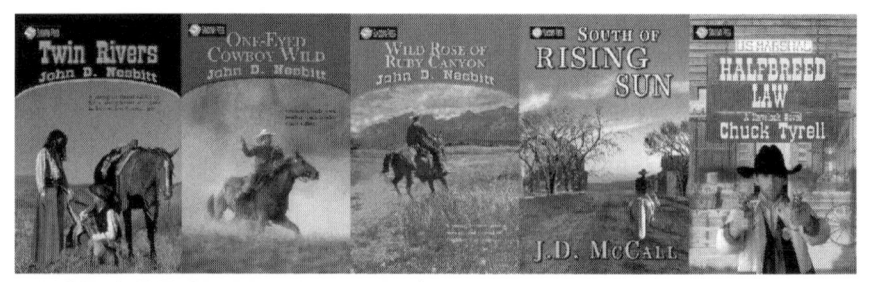

ONCE A DROVER—Jerry Guin
TRIPLE SHOT WESTERNS—John Nesbitt, Kevin Crisp, and Les Williams
ONE-EYED COWBOY WILD—John Nesbitt
TWIN RIVERS—John Nesbitt
WILD ROSE OF RUBY CANYON— John Nesbitt
HALFBREED LAW—Chuck Tyrell
SOUTH OF RISING SUN—John McCall
SUNDOWN WESTERN TALES—Max Brand, Charlie Steel, Zane Grey, Gordon L. Rottman, Richard Prosch, Kyle Rudek, W.M. Shockley, Robert Steele, Big Jim Williams, and Lane Pierce
THE DOCTOR'S BAG: MEDICINE AND SURGERY OF YESTERYEAR—Dr. Keith Souter
THE DUNDEE SAGA, BOOK 1: TUCSON—Kit Prate
THE DUNDEE SAGA, BOOK 2: CASA GRANDE—Kit Prate
THE OUTLAW, BILLY STARBUCK—Kit Prate

Printed in Poland
by Amazon Fulfillment
Poland Sp. z o.o., Wrocław